WINGS OF ICE

G. BAILEY

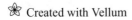 Created with Vellum

MORE BOOKS BY G. BAILEY

HER GUARDIANS SERIES

HER FATE SERIES

PROTECTED BY DRAGONS SERIES

LOST TIME ACADEMY SERIES

THE DEMON ACADEMY SERIES

DARK ANGEL ACADEMY SERIES

SHADOWBORN ACADEMY SERIES

DARK FAE PARANORMAL PRISON SERIES

SAVED BY PIRATES SERIES

THE MARKED SERIES

HOLLY OAK ACADEMY SERIES

THE ALPHA BROTHERS SERIES

A DEMON'S FALL SERIES

THE FAMILIAR EMPIRE SERIES

FROM THE STARS SERIES

THE FOREST PACK SERIES

THE SECRET GODS PRISON SERIES

THE REJECTED MATE SERIES

FALL MOUNTAIN SHIFTERS SERIES

ROYAL REAPERS ACADEMY SERIES

THE EVERLASTING CURSE SERIES

THE MOON ALPHA SERIES

CONTENTS

DESCRIPTION

**Four Dragon Guards. Three Curses. Two Heirs.
One Choice...
Forbidden love or the throne of the dragons?**

Isola Dragice thought she knew what her future
would bring. Only, one earth-shattering moment
destroys everything.

When war threatens her home, Isola returns from
earth to the world of dragons she knows nothing
about, and to Dragca Academy.
When the four most powerful dragon guards in
history are ordered to protect her, they didn't expect
to be protecting an accident prone princess. One who,

accidentally, nearly kills her whole class at Dragca Academy in her first week.

What happens when fire falls for Ice?

This story follows the Her Guardian Universe from a new point of view.

DEDICATION

For those who love cliffhangers (or hate them) this is for you.

PROLOGUE

Everything inside me screams as I run through the doors of the castle, seeing the dead dragons lining the floors, the view making me sick to my stomach. I try not to look at the spears in their stomachs, the dragonglass that is rare in this world. *Where did they get it?* The more and more bodies I pass, both dragon and guards, the less hope I have that my father is okay. *No, I can't be too late, I can't lose him, too.* The once grand doors to the throne room are smashed into pieces of stone, in a pile on the floor, and only the hinges to the door still hang on the walls. I run straight over, climbing over the rocks and broken stone. The sight in front of me makes me stop, not believing what I'm seeing, but I know it's true.

"Father . . .?" I plead quietly, knowing he won't reply to me. My father is sitting on his throne, a sword through his stomach, and an open-mouthed expression on his face. His blood drips down onto the gold floors of the throne room, and snow falls from the broken ceiling onto his face. There's no ice in here, no sign he even tried to fight before he was killed. He must not have seen it coming; he trusted whoever killed him.

"No," is all I can think to say as I fall to my knees, bending my head and looking down at the ground instead of at the body of my father. *I couldn't stop this, even after he warned me and risked everything.* I hear footsteps in front of me as I watch my tears drip onto the ground, but I don't look up. I know who it is. I know from the way they smell, my dragon whispers to me their name, but I can't even think it.

"Why?" I ask, even as everything clicks into place. I should have known; I should have never trusted him.

"Because the curse has to end. Because he was no good for Dragca. Our city needs a true heir, me. I'm the heir of fire and ice, the one the prophecy speaks of, and it's finally time I took what is mine," he says, and every word seems to cut straight through my heart. *I trusted him.*

"The curse hasn't ended, I'm still here," I whisper to the dragon in front of me, but I know he can hear my words as if I had just spoken them into his ear.

"Not for long, not even for a moment longer, actually. Your dragon guard will only thank me when you are gone. I didn't want to do this to you, not in the end, but you are too powerful. You are of no use to me anymore, not unless you're gone," he says. I look down at the ground as his words run around my head, and I don't know what to do. I feel lost, powerless, and broken in every way possible. There's a piece of the door in front of me that catches my attention, a part with the royal crest on it. The dragon in a circle, a proud, strong dragon. My father's words come back to me, and I know they are all I need to say.

"There's a reason ice dragons hold the throne and have for centuries. There is a reason the royal name Dragice is feared," I say and stand up slowly, wiping my tears away.

"We don't give up, and we bow to no one. I'm Isola Dragice, and you will pay for what you have done," I tell him as I finally meet his now cruel eyes, before calling my dragon and feeling her take over.

"Isola!" I hear shouted from the stairs, but I keep my headphones on as I stare at my laptop, and pretend I didn't hear her shout my name for the tenth time. The music blasts around my head as I try to focus on the history paper that is due tomorrow.

"Isola, will you take those things out and listen to me?" Jules shouts at me again, and I pop one of my headphones out as I look up at her. She stands at the end of my bed, her hands on her hips, and her glasses perched on the end of her nose. Her long grey hair is up in a tight bun, and she has an old-style dress that looks like flowers threw up on it. Jules is my house sitter, or babysitter as I like to call her. I don't think I need a babysitter at seventeen, not when I'm eighteen in a while anyway, and can look after myself.

"Both headphones out, I want them both out while you listen to me," she says. I knew this was coming. I pull the headphones out and pause the music on my phone.

"I did try to clean up after the party, I swear," I say, and she raises her eyebrows.

"How many teenagers did you have in here? Ten? A hundred?" she says, and I shrug my shoulders as I sit up on the bed and cross my legs.

"I don't know, it's all a little fuzzy," I reply honestly. My head is still pounding; it was probably the wine, or maybe the tequila shots. *Who knows?* I look up again as she shakes her head at me, speaking a sentence in Spanish that she knows I can't understand, but I doubt it's nice. I don't think I want to hear what she has to say about the party I threw last night anyway. I look around my simple room, seeing the dressing table, the wardrobe, and the bed I'm sitting on. There isn't much in here that is personal, no photos or anything that means anything to me.

"Miss Jules, looking as beautiful as always," Jace says, in an overly sweet tone as he walks into my bedroom. He walks straight over to Jules and kisses her cheek, making her giggle. Jace is that typical hot guy, with his white-blonde hair and crystal-blue eyes. Even my sixty-year-old house sitter can't be mad at him for long, he can charm just about anyone.

"Don't start with that pouty cute face," she tuts at him, and he widens his arms, pretending to be shocked.

"What face? I always look like this," he says, and she laughs, any anger she had disappearing.

"I'm going to clean up this state of a house, and you should leave, you're going to be late for school. I don't want to have to tell your father that as well, when I tell him about the party," she says, pointing a finger at me, and I have to hold in the urge to laugh. She emails my father all the time about everything I do, but he never responds. He just pays her to keep the house running and to make sure I don't get into too much trouble. If he hasn't had the time to talk to me in the last ten years, I doubt he's going to have the time to email a human he hired. Jules walks out of the room, and Jace leans against the wall, tucking his hands into his pockets. I run my eyes over his tight jeans, his white shirt that has ridden up a little to show his toned stomach, and finally to his handsome face that is smirking at me. *He knows exactly what he does to me.*

"You look too sexy when you do that," I comment, and he grins.

"Isn't that the point? Now come and give your boyfriend a kiss," he teases, and I fake a sigh before getting up and walking over to him. I lean up, brushing my lips against his cold ones, and he smiles, kissing me back just as gently.

"We should go, but I was wondering if you wanted to go to the mountains this weekend and try some flying?" he asks. I blank my expression before walking away from him and towards the mirror hanging on the wall near the door. I smooth my wavy, shoulder-length blonde hair down, and it just bounces back up, ignoring me. My blue eyes stare back at me, bright and crystal-clear. Jace says it's like looking into a mirror when he looks into my eyes, they are so clear. I check out my jeans and tank top, and grab my leather coat from where it hangs on the back of the door before answering Jace.

"I've got a lot of homework to do–" I say, and he shakes his head as he cuts me off.

"Issy, when was the last time you let her out? It's been, what, months?" he asks, and I turn away, walking out through my bedroom door and hearing him sigh behind me.

"Issy, we can't avoid this forever. Not when we

have to go back in two weeks," he reminds me, and I stop, leaning my head back against the plain white walls of the corridor.

"I know we have to go back. We have to train to rule a race we know nothing about, just because of who our parents are. Don't you ever want to run away, hide in the human world we have been left in all these years?" I ask, feeling a grumble of anger from my dragon inside my mind. I quickly slam down the barrier between me and my dragon in my head, stopping her from contacting me, no matter how much it hurts me to do so. *I can't let her control me.*

"Issy, we were left here so we would be safe. We are the last ice dragons, and our parents had no choice. Plus . . . being a dragon around humans is a nightmare, you know that," he says, stepping closer to me.

"I don't want to rule; I don't want anything to do with Dragca," I say, looking away.

"I guess it's lucky we have each other, ruling on our own would have been a disaster," he says, stepping in front of me so I can't move and gently kissing my forehead.

"I know. I just don't want to go back to see my father and everything that has to come with it," I say, and he steps back to tilt my head up to look at him.

"You're the heir to the throne of the dragons. You're the princess of Dragca. Your life was never meant to be lived here, with the humans," he says, and I move away from him, not replying because I know he sees it differently than I do. He is the ice prince, and his parents call him every week until they disappeared when he was twelve and he knows they loved him. I haven't spoken to any of my family in ten years, and I have never stepped back into Dragca since then. It's the only thing we disagree on, our future.

"Issy, let's just have a good day, and then, maybe, I could get you that peanut bacon sandwich you love from the deli?" he suggests, running to catch up with me on the stairs.

"Now you're talking," I grin at him as he hooks an arm around my waist, and leans down to whisper in my ear.

"And maybe later, I could do that thing with my tongue that you–" he gets cut off when Jules opens the door in front of us, clearing her throat, and ushering us out as we laugh.

"LITTLE ISSY, are you coming to my party this weekend? I know I'd love to show you my house and–" Michael asks as he stops me outside my English class, but I'm not listening to whatever he is saying. When I hear the bell ring, relief that it's the last class of the day fills me. Learning human things all day isn't fun, especially when you know you won't ever need to know any of it. The only class I love is my study period, where I can go to the library and find a new book to live in. I lift my bag on my shoulder and look around Michael for Jace, not seeing him anywhere. I look down at my arm as Michael steps closer, and he strokes a hand down it, making me shiver, but not in the good way.

"I don't know, I would have to ask Jace and see if he wants to go, but I don't think he likes you. Also, I'm not little, short is a better word," I say plainly, wanting to get as far away from Michael as possible. Michael is a good-looking human with black hair and is covered in tattoos, which I usually find attractive, but my dragon still wants to eat him, so even being friends with him would be a disaster. Plus, Jace would kill him if he saw how Michael was touching my arm. Dragons see their future mates as treasures, precious, and they don't share often.

"He doesn't own you; you could come alone,"

Michael snaps, clearly not happy I don't want to sneak off to his stupid frat-boy party.

"Why would I do that?" I ask the idiot football player, as I try to move away. I shove his hand off my arm, turning and walking away before he can reply.

"Because you're so much better than him. Come to my party!" he shouts at me, and everyone stops to look at us. They begin whispering, stupid rumours that will spread around the school by tomorrow. I don't even know Michael really, he's just another human I grew up with, and I know he isn't acting like himself. It's the dragon side of me that is attracting him, and every male human in this damn school. That's why I have always stayed close to Jace's side; male dragons have the opposite effect on humans. All the humans are scared of him here, everyone except for Jules. I stand on my tiptoes as I look around, before remembering Jace's last class was sports management on the other side of the building. I walk out of the school, going around the main entrance and see the gym across the field. I walk slowly across it, just thinking he must have had a shower or something after class, and he is running late. I stop dead in my tracks when I pick up an unfamiliar scent in the mixture of human smells. I smell a dragon, a fire dragon that shouldn't be here.

"Let me out," my dragon hisses in my mind. I slam the barrier down again, holding my head when she fights me, making me have to stop running towards the gym.

"Enough, Jace needs me!" I shout at her in my head, and she stops fighting instantly as she realises that I won't let her out and I can't help Jace like this. Overwhelming worry for Jace is the only thing coming from her as I run, and it floods my own emotions, nearly strangling me with panic. I run towards the door, push it open, and run across the small room that leads to the gym. I open the doors and immediately freeze at the sight in front of me, until a loud scream rips from my throat, and I fall to my knees. Even then, I can't believe it, not until the pain threatens to strangle me, not until I can't see anything other than the truth that is lying right in front of me.

"NO!" I scream out, my dragon's roar following my words as her sorrow and shock mixes with mine. In the middle of the room is Jace, a large red dagger sticking out of his heart, his head is fallen to the side, facing me with wide eyes in the dimly-lit room. I can't look away from his eyes, open in shock as blood drips from his mouth and makes a tiny noise as it hits the floor. I force myself to look away from his eyes, only to look at the blood that makes a circle around him, so much blood that pours from the wound. I crawl across the gym floor, tears running from my eyes, and I don't stop, even as my hands get covered in his blood once I get to him. I pull his head onto my lap, stroking a blood-stained finger across his cheek.

"No! Jace, baby, wake up. Please don't do this to me," I plead, my hand shaking against his cheek as he remains still. I know he is dead, my dragon and I both know it, but I can't believe it. Everything in me feels like it's breaking into a million pieces. I hear footsteps behind me, but I can't look away from Jace, as I raise my hand and close his eyes, leaving bloody finger-prints on his eyelids. I take a deep breath, committing to memory the smell of the fire dragon that did this to Jace.

"I vow revenge, I vow to never let this be forgotten. I will always love you," I whisper, my tears falling onto his face as I press my forehead to his, and then scream and scream, until my throat cracks.

"Don't. Let her say goodbye, we have time," I hear a male voice say behind me. I turn and look over my shoulder, the shock from everything just seeming to merge together as I see my father standing at the door. Ten royal guards stand around him, and his ice-blue eyes watch me. There's no sorrow or remorse in my father's eyes, not that I honestly expected anything else from him.

"Time to leave, there is nothing to be done here, Isola," he tells me. I look back at Jace, not wanting to let him go, but knowing my father's suggestion to leave wasn't really a suggestion at all. I have to go; whoever did this to Jace would kill me in a heartbeat.

"Isola, we must leave. Danger is near," my father warns me once more, and I gently rest Jace's body on the floor.

"I love you, and I'm so sorry I wasn't here. That I couldn't save you," I whisper. As I lean down and kiss Jace's cold cheek, another sob escapes me, and I wipe my eyes.

"Give him a true dragon's burial, or I will not leave," I warn my father as I stand up, blood sticking to both my clothes and my hands. I step back, seeing a young guard my age come to stand next to me. I look up into his hazel eyes, the only part of his body that I can see, thanks to the black uniform that covers his head and all of his body. The only other colour is the ice-blue dragon crest over his heart. All the dragon guards wear uniforms like this in the human world, and what I remember of them in Dragca is not much different.

"You have my vow," he says, and something

makes me believe him as we stare at each other. I step back, turning and walking over to my father after one last look at Jace. My father stands tall as he holds a hand out for me, like I'm a child that needs his comfort. I ignore his hand and stand in front of him, feeling the dragon guards close ranks around us.

"I am sorry we were late, we didn't know of the threat until it was too late," he says. I don't say a word, I can't. Jace is dead; my dragon mate and the dragon I was meant to marry. We should have run away, not stayed here.

"What will be done now? There are no ice dragons other than you and me," I comment, needing to focus on anything other than the broken feeling in my heart, as the smell of smoke fills the air. The dragon guard will be burning Jace's body, and the thought makes me want to crumble onto the ground.

"Remember that our bodies are just shells for our dragons, that Jacian will be free to fly the night skies, and you will see him again one day," my father offers advice, and I still stand completely silent. I watch tiny red sparks float into the air around the gym, the soul of Jace leaving this world. They disappear slowly; each time they go, it shatters me a little bit. *No words will take away the pain that is crushing my heart.*

TWO

"Tell me, what happened today? How did Jacian end up dead?" my father asks me in a disappointed tone, as we walk through the forest behind my home and towards the portal to Dragca. I look down at my red coat, wondering which student the guard stole it from as I pull it closer around myself. I look down at my still blood-covered hands, Jace's blood, and I almost trip on a rock as the image of his dead body flashes into my head. *He is really gone.*

"Why don't you tell me why you are here early? Did you know this would happen?" I ask him, knowing it's no coincidence that he turned up early, just as Jace was killed. *My Jace is gone.* As I wipe more tears away, I think about how I won't be able to kiss him again, how I won't be waking up next to him anymore. The boy I grew up with, fell in love with . . . is gone.

"I asked first," he replies, and I turn to look over at him as he walks at my side. My father's white hair is cut short, his white crown sparkles in the sun. He has a black cloak that slides across the ground, with blue embroidered edges and the dragon crest on the chest. He looks every bit the king I remember, but not my father.

"Nothing abnormal happened, it was a normal day," I reply, looking forward again, I feel the portal magic as we draw closer.

"What of Jules?" I ask, after he doesn't reply to me for a long time.

"Who?" he answers with a question, and I shake my head with a low laugh. I was right, he never read a single one of the hundreds of emails, or checked in on me once over the years. I used to pretend that he couldn't come to me because it wasn't safe, and that maybe he was watching me from a distance. Or talking to Jules about me. *I guess I was wrong.*

"The house sitter, the woman you left me with, the one who brought me up?" I ask, trying not to snap at him.

"Oh, we have left a decent amount of human money for her, she is now retired, which I'm sure she is happy about," he waves me off, clearly not caring at all.

"I wish I could have said goodbye," I say quietly.

"She is just a human, they would not care for goodbyes if they knew what you really are, Isola. Plus, we have bigger issues to focus on," he says, stopping the conversation, and I smile tightly. I'm guessing feelings are not something my father cares about.

"Fine. How did you know we were going to be attacked?" I ask him.

"The royal seer had a vision, a dragon death, but I didn't know which one of you or what time it would be. We came as soon as possible," he replies, his tone is so calm, as he talks about his only child possibly dying, or the man she was due to mate with. I look away as tears start slowly falling down my cold cheeks, wiping them on my coat.

"You must not cry anymore, you must be strong as we return to Dragca. Enemies watch us at all times," he scolds me as I continue to cry. A feeling of numbness spreads over me, just holding myself together until I can be alone and let my feelings out. He has a point, I know my life is in danger, and I can't die now. Jace will have died for nothing if I die, too, and no one would remember him like I do.

"You can't tell me how to feel," I snap, feeling my dragon weeping in my mind. She doesn't even try to contact me anymore, just sits quietly, and that is very unlike her. She feels like I do, broken, and I don't put the barrier up between us, letting her emotions mix with my own.

"I am not telling you what to feel, only how to act. You are Isola Dragice. The powerful princess we have waited for," he grabs my arm to stop me walking. "Act like it. Don't shame Jace's memory," he tells me firmly, and all the guards stop to wait for us as we stare at each other. I look into my father's frosty blue eyes, the coldness of them having nothing to do with the ice dragon inside of him. He is just cold-hearted, just like I remember him being. I never had the loving father, and I don't expect that from him now. It still stings that he demands what I do, how I should act, when he knows nothing of me.

"Are we going to the castle?" I ask, changing the subject, and shoving his hand off my arm. He pauses, looking down at me strangely for a second, before turning away.

"No, we are going to Dragca Academy. The castle

is not safe enough for you at the moment. The academy is, and you must learn about your world before you take the throne," he says, making me go silent. It was never the plan to go to Dragca Academy; a school full of fire dragons is no place for an ice dragon like me.

"Father, I was meant to take the throne in two weeks, what has changed?" I ask.

"I will explain more when we get to Dragca," he replies, looking around at the dragon guards. I nod in understanding. He doesn't want to tell me when so many of the dragon guard could hear. I pause as I spot the portal, a yellow wall that shimmers in between some tall trees that look like all the others here. Humans cannot see it, and even if they got close, the portal naturally pushes them away. It makes them want to get away from it at all costs, even scaring the weak-minded humans. Some humans with strong minds have made it through the portal, but they can never find a way to return, and life in Dragca as a human isn't easy.

"In formation, the king and princess follow two guards through, and the others behind," a guard next to my father shouts, and we get into a line at his command. The guard in front whispers to the portal, telling it where we need to go. The guards keep their swords at their sides as we each walk towards the barrier. My father steps through in front of me, and I stop, freezing as a memory of when I last went through a portal flitters into my mind.

"You have to let go now," my father says, as I clutch his hand tightly and force myself to let go. He walks through the portal, and I follow, trying not to jump at the cold feeling. I pull my cloak closer around myself as I walk towards my father where he is speaking with two guards.

"Take her to the house, and then travel a fair distance away before coming back to Dragca," he tells the guards. I look up at the snow falling from the sky, it lands on my nose, and I wipe it away as I wait.

"Go with them, Isola," my father tells me, not even looking my way, as he walks around me and towards the portal.

"Wait! Father, what is going on? Where are you going?"

"I have a world to rule, and you must stay here, stay alive. We will see each other again, Isola, and I will send information with the ice prince," he says,

and I run after him only to be caught by a guard and picked up.

"Father, don't leave me like mother, please don't!" I scream, wiggling and trying to get the guard to put me down. My father looks back at me one more time, no compassion or anything loving for me to remember, as he disappears. I realize that not only did I lose my mother that year, but also my father.

"YOUR HIGHNESS?" a guard says, pressing a hand on my shoulder, and I quickly shake myself out of the memory that haunted me for years, the heartless father who left me here in the human world and acted like I was forgotten. Jace was sent to me a few months later, with boxes of books and information on dragons. He got me to leave my room for the first time in a long time. He made me laugh, and explained that my father only did what he did to keep me safe. I step through the portal, feeling the cold magic push against my body, and then I open my eyes to the home I've not seen since I was eight.

Dragca Academy is right in the middle of the snowy mountains, and the only way to get in is to use a portal or fly. The academy, itself, is a huge castle with three towers, three levels of balconies for dragons to land on. There is a stone path leading to the doors, a side building with a stone battle field outside, which is covered in weapons in metal holders. There is what looks like an arena behind the castle, but I can't tell from here. I spot three other dragons walking around and one flying over the mountains in the distance, but they are only shadows from here. I look up at the stars, knowing it must be late here. Time is opposite on Earth and Dragca, as are the seasons and just about everything you can think of. Dragca has two suns and two moons in the sky. I look around to see the two moons, the large one and the tiny one by its side.

"My King," a woman says, distracting me from staring, and I turn around to see her walking down the steps of the castle. She has a dark-blue cloak on, the royal crest on a silver pin holding the cloak together. She lowers the hood, her long dark-red hair falling around her shoulders. She smiles widely as I try to think why she looks so familiar to me.

"Esmeralda, it is a pleasure to see you. You're as beautiful as I remember," my father says, taking her hand and kissing it, and I mentally roll my eyes when she laughs sweetly at him.

"It has been many years since you married my

sister, and yet you are still the charmer," she says, making me remember why she looks so familiar now. She is my step-aunt and the headmaster of Dragca Academy, if I remember right. I remember them being called the ice and fire twins, one born of ice and the other of fire. A rare birth in our world, nearly impossible, and apparently it shocked all of Dragca. I read about them in one of the books my father left, as I was interested in the stepmother I had only met two months before I was sent to Earth. All I remember about her is her long, perfect white hair, and how cruel she was to the maids and dragon guards in the castle. My father married her not long after my mother died because she was the last female ice dragon alive other than me. They soon found out she couldn't have children, making me and Jace the only heirs to the throne left. The only ice dragons left. Now there are three: my father, me, and my stepmother.

"And yet you still look as beautiful as all those years ago. My wife sends her love," he says, and she rests her hand on his arm in an overly affectionate way. I'm pretty sure my stepmother wouldn't like that her sister seems so familiar with her husband. But then, I don't really know anything about them.

"Come in, we have a lot to discuss. Where is Jacian?" she asks, her eyes finally landing on me.

"Dead," I reply, almost robotically, as I stand completely still.

Esmeralda's hand flies to her mouth, "I am so sorry, Isola."

Part of me believes her, but I can't think about it. I look away as we all start walking quietly towards the castle. I blink and do a double take when I see a man standing in the shadows under one of the towers. He's dressed in all black, and I'm sure he is a guard, but for some reason, I can't stop staring at him as he moves closer. He lifts his hand, and I catch a glint of silver before he throws it at us.

"Get down!" I scream, slamming into my father, and we fall to the ground as the dagger lands in the heart of the guard on his right. The guard falls to the ground in front of us, as the other guards form a tight circle around us and pull their swords out. The guards quickly make a circle of fire around them, the heat blasting against my skin.

"Five to the left, two on the right," my father says, sniffing the air.

"When I say the word, run to the doors and get inside," my father tells me. He grabs my chin with his hand when I don't answer, "Do you understand, Isola?" he asks, and I nod despite the shock.

"Now!" he shouts, throwing his hands in the air and shooting ice in every direction except the one I'm running in. Ice and dragonglass, are the only ways to kill a fire dragon easily. Fire cannot kill an ice dragon, that is what makes us different and stronger. Only dragonglass can–and our own ice, not that we would use our ice on ourselves. *That wouldn't be smart*. The fire wall parts when I get close, closing behind me as I run straight to the closed stone doors.

"Duck, princess!" I hear a man shout from my left, and I turn my head to see a man dressed in the all-black guard uniform running at me. He has black hair that's cut short and shaved at the sides, his lip is pierced with a ring, and the man is built like an actual god. *Or like a rock star from Earth*. I'm too busy staring at the guy to stop him when he slams into me, both of us landing on the floor as a dagger flies past us.

"What part of 'duck' do you not understand?" the man asks, rolling us over, so he is on top of me. He looks down at me, placing his hands near my head as he rolls his lip ring between his lips, somehow frowning at me at the same time.

"Get the hell off of me, who do you think you are?" I ask him, watching as he smirks at me.

"Dagan Fire, nice to meet you princess. Now stay down, or I might as well kill you, myself," he says as he jumps off me in a fluid motion, pulling a red dagger out of his belt and throwing it. I roll on to my stomach to see the dagger land in the forehead of one of the attackers, and the body slams to the floor. When I turn back over, Dagan holds a hand out for me.

"You don't have to say thank you," he says as I accept his hand to pull me up.

"I was going to," I reply, and he grins, still holding my hand as we stare at each other.

"I am one of the dragon guard, your kind doesn't say thank you to us. We die for you royals every day. We are just soldiers, and soldiers don't get thanked as they die," he says, giving me a sarcastic smirk as he drops my hand and steps away. I watch him look around, following his gaze to the five dragon guards lying dead, some from my father's ice that is every-where, and others from dragonglass daggers.

"Now get inside, princess," Dagan demands, pissing me off, and I step closer, looking up at him.

"Dagan Fire, thank you for saving my life, but if you tell me what to do again, we will have a big problem," I tell him, and before he can reply, my father steps next to me. Dagan looks away, his jaw grinding in annoyance.

"Bring the bodies inside, I want to know who dares to attack the king and princess," he tells Dagan, who nods as he steps back and turns around. My father puts his hand on my back as he walks us inside the castle, and I don't look back once.

"My office is this way," Esmeralda says, waving a hand towards a corridor in the middle of the entryway we have walked into. There are two staircases on each side that lead to the next level, and everything in here is different shades of gold and brown. The brown wooden floors Are made of the same wood as the staircases. There are gold walls, which are empty of any decoration, and gold chandeliers light up the corridor. *There must be like ten of them in this space alone, talk about overkill.* We walk down the long corridor, until we get to the end where there is a set of double doors.

"Wait outside," my father tells the guards, who each nod their heads in submission, before he walks in the room. I walk in last, shutting the door behind me as I have a look around. There is a giant desk in front of two windows that overlook a field, the arena, and the mountains. There are some chairs, a bookcase, and little else in here.

"Please sit," Esmeralda says, as she takes her seat behind the desk, and my father sits in one of the two chairs in front of it. I sit down in the spare chair, crossing my legs and raising my eyebrow at my father who sighs.

"We are at war; the fire dragon rebellion has raised an army. Every day, more and more people are siding with them because of the seers," he says, and I lean back in my seat in shock. That was not what I expected him to say to me, not one tiny bit of what he said. I knew a fire dragon killed my mother years ago, setting a dragon hunt on the fire dragons to find out who did it. Everyone loved my mother, she was a good queen who helped the poor and innocent. She made laws that helped them, opened orphanages and even adopted several dragon children, keeping them in the castle and teaching them in her spare time. No one knew why anyone would kill her, and the seers never saw it.

"The seers? Why would more fire dragons side

with the rebellion because of the seers?" I ask confused.

"We have the royal seer locked up because she keeps trying to escape, and the whole of the seer village has joined the fire dragon rebellion," he says with an angry growl following his statement. There is a royal seer family, from what I remember reading, who lived in the castle, but I don't remember them as a child. It's likely I never met them.

"Why don't you give her up? Let her go, and maybe the seers–"

"Enough. Do not tell me what to do, Isola. There is far more you do not understand, and we cannot give up the young seer. She is too powerful, and it was her mother that made the prophecy that started the war in the first place," he says, speaking of the prophecy that was made the day I was born. I've heard of it from Jace, but I never listened to what he had to say. I don't believe that everything is destined to be, seers can be wrong.

"If I was to let her go free, and she has a vision as powerful as her mother's, it would just feed their army and make more people side with them," my father sighs.

"No one believes that prophecy, right?" I ask, but my father doesn't look at me. I don't even remember all of it, something about fire falling for ice or something.

"Remind me of it, it's been years since I've heard it," Esmeralda cuts in, looking between us, and I sit back in my seat.

"When fire falls for ice, Dragca will bear the price.
Ice and fire will destroy the curses, but a new curse
will be born.
Only ice can stop the fire that spreads . . . .
The fire that will destroy . . . .
The fire that will burn eternal.
Ice must fall for fire, just as fire must fall for ice.
Sides will be chosen with blood, death will show the
way through death.
Only fire must win . . . .
The heir of ice and fire must rule . . . ."

My father recites the prophecy, and none of us say a word as we think it over. Seers can be wrong, most of the time they are, but never wrong about everything. Some parts of the prophecy must come true, if not all of it, and none of it makes any sense to me. I assume it means a fire dragon falling for an ice dragon, but I don't see that happening anytime soon. I also don't see how fire must win. It makes no sense.

"Who is the heir of ice and fire?" I ask the only question I can think of.

"No one, they don't exist," my father snaps and then puts a hand on my shoulder.

"You are the only heir of Dragca. I don't have any siblings, and I never had another child," he tells me what I already know, but he looks at me until I nod, relief spreading over his face as he leans back.

"Can't our army stop the fire dragons?" I say, thinking of the large army my father has, full of dragon guards.

"We can't get to them, Isola, but we are looking for a way, and we will destroy the rebellion before you take the throne. I will not hand you a kingdom at war," he says, growls from his dragon following his word. I see frost escaping his fingers and sliding down the arm of the chair. He must be angry to lose control like that. The chair creaks, threatening to snap from the ice.

"What now?" I eventually ask when he has calmed down a little.

"You will stay here, and your uncle will watch over you. He has been appointed the new headmaster of Dragca Academy," he says, shocking me with an uncle I barely remember. I remember Jace telling me about him, how my grandmother adopted him at a young age. That's why he is a fire dragon, and not ice like my mother.

"Uncle? My mother's brother?" I ask, thinking back to the man with fiery red hair I remember as a child.

"Yes, he is a fantastic fighter, a smart dragon, and he will be a good mentor for you," he tells me.

"And Esmeralda?" I ask, looking over at her as she smiles at me.

"I am to return to the castle to protect my sister. The castle isn't safe, and my family needs me," she replies before my father can.

"Why now? Is it because I was meant to take the throne with Jace? When they find out he is dead, and there is no way for me to take the throne without an ice dragon mate—" I start rambling.

"Enough," my father cuts me off.

"But—"

"There is a reason the royal name Dragice is feared, there is a reason ice dragons have held the throne for thousands of years. You are Isola Dragice, and they will bow to you because Dragice dragons bow to no one. They will see you as their true queen, with or without a king, or I will finish them," he says, the promise coming through his words as more ice leaves his hand, until the whole chair is frozen, and his eyes are completely white. He must be close to shifting into his dragon, and the loss of control of his gifts says it all about the anger he is feeling. I want to think he might even be worried about me, my future, but his emotionless expression makes me feel like he is more frightened about losing the throne.

"I understand," I tell him quietly, and his eyes return back to their normal colour.

"I will take you to your room before I leave," Esmeralda tells me, and I nod at her as I stand up.

"Come here," my father opens his arms as he stands as well, and I step into a hug from him. It feels weird to be held by my father, as I can't remember him ever holding me, even as a child. He was always busy, always had many other things he needed to do.

"Be strong, there is so much of both me and your mother inside of you. Don't let death destroy your heart, and we will see each other in six months, for the winter solstice," he whispers to me. I want to agree with him, but you can't destroy something that is already broken, and my heart is too broken to be destroyed. I don't reply to him as I step out of his arms and walk over to the door that Esmeralda opens. The guards move to the side, two of them following us, and the others staying with my father.

"I'm sure your uncle will want to see you first

thing in the morning. I will speak to the remaining dragon guards to work out a way for a guard to be with you at all times," she tells me as we get to the right staircase and start walking up. I don't reply to her, I just keep walking silently, wanting to get to my room and shut the door on the world.

"I am sorry for your loss, I know how crushing it is to lose your mate at a young age," she tells me, and I turn my head to look up at her as she continues to talk. I can't think about Jace right now without bursting into tears, which is not something I can do when I need to be strong right now. Jace wouldn't want me to break down.

"Can we talk about something else?" I ask as we pass two girls. One has long ginger hair and the other black with red tips. They both stare at me for way too long—actually stop walking to stare. I try not to let it bother me, I'm used to humans being weird around me growing up. They might not actually know what is different about me, like the dragons here do, but humans aren't stupid, they can sense something.

"I was promised to a fire dragon at ten, and we grew up together, fell in love at fifteen. The day before our mating ceremony, your mother was killed, and he was one of the dragons who fought to protect her. Losing his life doing so," she tells me, not exactly changing the subject, as she is trying to relate to me in some way, but I do feel sorry for her.

"I didn't realise guards died trying to protect my mother, I thought the attacker caught everyone off guard when he snuck into the castle and killed her," I say, remembering the bells going off in the castle that night. It's one of the only things I remember like it was yesterday. My father woke me up, hiding me in the secret passageways with royal guards. I remember him coming back for me hours later, covered in my mother's blood, and he told me she was gone. I screamed at him, ran to my mother's room, and stared at her dead body on the bed for hours before a guard picked me up and took me away.

"Five guards died trying to stop him—I knew them all—they were good men. As much as your mother was a good queen who didn't deserve to die as she did," she says, and we get to the top of the staircase.

"I was glad when your father found the betrayer and killed him for what he did, though I am sorry that many fire dragons were killed to find the attacker," she says, and I agree with her. I can't wait to find out who killed Jace, because I won't stop until I do. I will train and become strong enough to kill the person that took him from me, there isn't any other option.

"This way," she points at one of the three corridors. We walk down to the bottom of it, which stretches into a longer straight passageway with dozens of wooden doors.

"This is yours," Esmeralda says, pointing at the fifth door in the row and walking over, unlocking it with a key that she hands me after opening the door.

"Please try not to lose the key, they are a nightmare to replace," she tells me as I slide the key into my coat pocket and walk into the large bedroom after her. The room is circular in shape, with another door to the left of me, a round bed in the middle, and a small window with a window seat. There's a storage trunk at the end of the bed and a cream rug in front of it.

"The bathroom is through there, and the morning begins at seven am, Monday to Friday. The weekends are yours to study or socialize," she says, walking past me to the door as I stop in the middle of the room.

"The guards will bring your suitcase up, I'm sure," she says and then surprises me as she shuts the door with the guard on the other side. She walks over to me, placing her hands on my shoulders, and keeping eye contact with me.

"Your father will tell you to lay low here, to be safe, and do as you are asked. Don't do that. You need to stand out, so the other dragons don't push you over. You need to make friends, so you are not alone. Most of all, you need to train every hour because this war isn't going to be over when your father wins. They will always want you dead, they will always want a fire dragon on the throne. Be smart, survive this, and get revenge on whoever killed Jacian," she says and steps away, looking nervously at the door and back to me.

"Why tell me this? Why help me?" I ask her.

"Because I was friends with your mother, she was kind to me when I lost everything. I will protect her child because I see so much of her in you, and you are the true heir. Even as young an heir as you are now, you have power. I believe dark times are coming for Dragca, and we need a true ruler," she says and walks out of the room, shutting the door behind her. I walk over to my bed, sitting down and pulling out my phone from my pocket. The battery is low, but I still get to stare at the photos of Jace, with tears running down my face until I pass out.

CHAPTER

FOUR

ISOLA

Ice and fire. Fire and ice. It's everywhere, swirling around a girl I cannot see in the middle of it. Four men are standing around her, protecting her I think.

"Fire and ice is your future," a girl's voice says behind me, and I quickly swirl around to see a shadow of a girl walking into the room.

"What?" I ask her.

"Fire and ice. Light and dark. Good and evil. They need each other, like you will need your guards, your four others," she says, her voice echoing around my mind as she repeats the sentence time and time again.

"Jace?" I call instinctively, as I roll over in my bed and open my eyes to the vacant spot next to me. It

41

takes a few seconds of staring at the empty space before the tears start to fall, and I roll over on my back, forgetting the strange dream to the reality that being awake is stranger. I look up at the unfamiliar ceilings, then over to the light that shines through the thin curtains, noticing the overwhelming scent of fire dragons around here. I feel around the bed, finding my phone and trying to turn it on, only to see it's flat. Looking at the room, I highly doubt I'm going to find a plug, much less my charger.

"Princess, your uncle wishes to see you before class, which starts in an hour," a young-sounding guard shouts after banging on the door. I don't reply as I put my phone on the side and seriously debate not getting out of bed at all.

"I have breakfast for you," he shouts again when I don't reply. My stomach grumbles before I can even think of rejecting the idea of food. I don't even remember when I ate last as I skipped breakfast yesterday, and then with everything that happened, food was the last thing on my mind.

"One minute," I shout back as I groan and slide out of bed. Every part of me wants to get back into it and not move, just sink into the blankets and forget my life. But there's one part, a part that makes me walk over to the bathroom and stare at myself in the mirror above the sink. The part that knows no one will avenge Jace if I get back into that bed. I look in the mirror at my eyes, watching as the pupil spreads out and turns silver as I whisper to my dragon.

"I know you're hurting like me, but I need you now, okay? Talk to me?" I ask, waiting for her to respond. She doesn't, I just get slammed with a whole load of pain from her that takes my breath away as I lean against the sink. I sigh as my eyes turn back to the normal blue, and I pick up the brand-new brush off the counter and sort my hair out. Once I'm done, I brush my teeth with the new toothbrush I find and come out of the bathroom, stopping in my tracks at the sight of the guard placing a bundle of clothes on my bed. He turns at the noise, looking at me with a small smile. The guard appears to be my age. He has short, wavy brown hair, and hazel eyes with a touch of red in them, like most fire dragons have. The redder, the more powerful they are, but the bloodlines have apparently been diluted over the years, so most dragons only have dots of red or little specks. I remember Jace telling me that, but at the time I didn't care or want to know about Dragca and its inhabitants. But I still remember everything Jace said to me.

"I'm Thorne Riverle, one of your personal guards. Here is the uniform you need to wear today and some breakfast, princess," he says, bowing low and straightening back up as I look him over. He is dressed in a uniform of tight black leather and is bare of weapons, which is odd for a dragon guard. The black trousers show off his impressive thighs, and the shirt is fitted, with a dip that puts his defined chest on display. A cloak is tied at his neck with a silver clip of the royal crest. I clear my throat when I realize how long I've just spent staring at him without speaking. *He must think I'm an idiot.*

"It's Issy, or Isola. I don't mind which you call me, but not 'princess' please, that's just weird," I say, making him chuckle a little. It's a damn sexy chuckle, too.

"Okay, Issy, I will wait outside to escort you to your uncle," he tells me, bowing once more before walking out of my room and shutting the door. As I watch him leave, I spot the suitcase by the door. I run over, pull it into the middle of the room and open it up. There's a bundle of clothes that someone has chucked in, a lot of it sexy lingerie. The idea of a guard looking at my underwear makes me cringe. There are two dresses, but mainly leggings and shirts. I keep searching for my Kindle or iPod, not finding either.

"Damn it," I grumble, knowing that my phone is

flat, and there is no way for me to read now. I was halfway through a damn good book before I had to stop reading to do that annoying thing called sleep. I toss all the clothes back in, deciding I will have to ask the guards about charging my phone, so I can use the Kindle app or something. I walk over and pick up the leather top and trousers and black cloak that is folded on my bed.

"Dear god, it's like Harry Potter dressed in leather," I mutter to myself. I put the clothes on, feeling them stick to my body like another layer of skin and then pull the cloak around my shoulders. I look at the food, knowing I should eat, but I don't want to. I don't know why, whether it's nerves or the image of Jace with the dagger through his stomach running through my mind, but pancakes and orange juice have never looked so horrible. I walk to the door, pulling it open and see Thorne waiting to the side. His eyes widen, then slowly make their way down my body before he seems to snap out of it. He quickly straightens and averts his eyes, though my cheeks still burn with embarrassment.

"The clothes suit you," he says as I shut the door and walk with him down the corridor. I don't reply as three girls pass us, all whispering as they look at me, and I just stare back. They don't even try to hide the fact they are talking about me, which I'm not sure whether to respect or hate. We walk past them, straight to the stairs in the middle of this corridor and go down.

"What is with all this leather?" I ask, feeling uncomfortable about how tight it is. I look over at him, noticing the leather outfits of the guards aren't too different from my own, but theirs covers from the neck down their arms, while mine has cold shoulder cutouts.

"It's magic-blessed leather made by the tree spirits," he says plainly, like I should know this, but I've never heard of them.

"Tree spirits?" I ask as we walk past another group of people who also stare and whisper. It's getting annoying now, but I don't know what exactly to say to them. I'm not like them, not really. Fire and ice couldn't be more different. I guess I never expected to be alone to deal with the fire dragons and their hate for my kind. I thought I'd have Jace at my side.

"Each tree has a spirit, that's who you speak to when you ask a portal to take you somewhere. They also make leather, which is blessed so that when you shift, it doesn't rip the clothes and they appear when you shift back. No one sees the tree spirits, they don't appear for dragons or humans anymore, but they will weave leather as gifts for the king," he explains. I've never heard of these tree spirits, but then, I never went to school in Dragca until now. Tree spirits aren't something you get taught about in human high school. I kinda wish it was, I doubt math is useful to me now.

"What do they look like?" I ask curiously.

"Pretty little dolls, with green hair and green skin. They are about the size of your hand, and known for causing mischief," he tells me.

"Sounds cute," I comment.

"Well, light tree spirits are, dark ones have blue hair, blue skin and are said to be a little less cute," he tells me as we move around a big group of students that are engrossed in conversation and don't even notice us.

"What do dark spirits do?" I ask.

"They are tree spirits as well, but they are born when a tree dies. No one knows much about them, to be honest. Most people don't even believe they exist," he says with an almost sad tone as we get to the door of the same office I was in last night. Three guards are standing motionless outside, until they see me and bow.

"I will wait for you here and take you to class," Thorne says with a formal bow as a guard knocks on the door and then opens it for me. I walk in, hearing the door shut behind me as I look at the back of my uncle, who stands looking out the window. He has a grey suit on, his dark-red hair with grey tips is a stark contrast. He waves a hand, beckoning me over.

"Do you remember my name? You were so young when I saw you last, Isola," he says; despite his words coming across as gentle, there's a touch of a snarl in his tone.

"No," I reply as he turns to look at me. His dark-red eyes lock with mine, but although I know he must be powerful, I am not frightened. He walks straight over to me, and I stand still as he moves around me in a circle, examining me.

"You look so much like my sister, it's like going back in time to when we were teenagers," he says, moving a hand to touch me before suddenly changing his mind, lowering his hand.

"I don't have any photos of her, only memories that I'm not sure are even real," I say.

"My name is Louis Pendragon, the last of the Pendragons, as you have the royal name, and I never had a child," he says, with no emotion in his tone. "You should get to your class, I only wished to look at you," he adds, walking away to sit down in his chair. I give him a confused look at being excused so quickly, but turn around, walking towards the door.

"One more thing, Isola," he says, stopping me when I get to the door.

"This is not the human world, nor do we play by their rules. I suggest you get your dragon on your side, otherwise you will be powerless to survive here," he comments.

"How did you know?" I ask, stunned.

"Leave, Isola," he commands, looking down at the paperwork in front of him, and he picks up a pen to start writing something.

"Goodbye, *uncle*," I say, making him flinch a little, and I walk out of the room.

CHAPTER
FIVE
ISOLA

"Did everything go well?" Thorne asks when I step outside the office. The guards shut the door behind me, moving back into their motionless stance.

"I actually have no idea," I mutter. I don't want to think about my complicated uncle and his strange ability to know that I'm not in control of my dragon, which I should be at my age. No one should know that, it's impossible, and I can't help but think about how he knew. My dragon is inside my mind, speaking only to me.

"Err, okay. So, this is the way to all of the classes, except for a few out buildings where training fights are held," he says, pointing to the left staircase as we walk back to the entrance hall. There are a few students walking around, carrying books, and wearing their hoods up, so I can't see their faces.

"To the right, are all the dorms, study rooms, and the library," he comments.

"Wait, there's a library?" I ask, grabbing his arm, and he looks at me strangely.

"Yes," he says slowly.

"That's the best damn thing I've heard all day," I say cheerily, and walk up the staircase with Thorne hurrying to catch up. At the top is a circle corridor, lined with lockers and classroom doors in between them.

"Lockers? Not what I expected," I tell Thorne, who reaches into his cloak and hands me another key, this one is small and blue. He pulls out a chain from his other pocket, hooking the key on.

"Hand me your room key, Issy?" he asks, holding out a hand. I feel around my cloak pocket until I find it, and hand it to him. He slides the key onto the chain and holds it out for me.

"Thanks," I say, taking it off him.

"It's just easier to have them on a small chain, it's nothing," he smiles and looks around.

"Yours is number one hundred, nice and easy to remember," he says, nodding his head to the left, and I walk just behind him. I stop when I see a guy leaning against the wall; even through all of the students, we just seem to lock eyes with each other. Thorne stops, walking back to my side, and looking at where I'm staring.

"That's the kind of dragon you want to stay away from, Issy," Thorne tells me, my eyes still locked on the almost black ones staring at me from across the hallway. I trail my eyes over his messy black hair, the long tips that brush over his forehead. I look down at his muscular arms crossed against his large chest before raising my eyes back to his. He is dressed in all leather, covered in tattoos, and I get the feeling Thorne is right.

"What's his name?" I ask Thorne.

"Elias Fire," Thorne grumbles, as Elias gets a cigarette out of his pocket and lights it up. He puts it in his mouth, sucking in slowly as he watches me like I watch him. His lips pull up in a sinful smirk before blowing the smoke out and walking away.

"I mean it when I say stay away from him; Elias Fire is nothing but dangerous. A killer that is dripping with dirty blood," Thorne sneers, and I have to agree with him. Elias looks just like everything any normal girl should avoid, and yet, I can't help but stare at him as he walks away.

"Is Dagan Fire his brother?" I ask Thorne, who is

watching Elias like I am, but my question makes him glance down at me. He looks furious, his eyes turning slightly black in the corner as his dragon threatens to take over.

"The Fire brothers are not guys you want to make friends with, Isola," he says and walks away, fists held tightly at his sides. I jog a little to catch up with him, and he stops at a door.

"This is yours, I will wait outside each class," he says coldly. I nod, sliding the key chain into my pocket, and walk to the door. I open it and walk in, seeing five other students sitting down, all of them at the front, and they all stare at me with wide eyes. I don't see the teacher in the small room, which is full of dark-brown benches and has a whiteboard at the front, with a desk in front of it. I walk through the students, seeing an empty desk with two seats right at the back, and sit down in it. For the next ten minutes, students rush in, and all pause to stare at me. I try to just ignore it, focusing on the empty whiteboard instead. No one sits next to me, which I'm thankful for.

"Morning, class, good to see most of you are awake today," a woman laughs as she walks into the room with a massive pile of books nearly touching her chin, and slams them down on her desk. She

smooths her blonde hair, which is pulled into a ponytail that highlights her dark-red tips. Pushing her
glasses up, she smiles brightly when she sees me.

"We have a new student, Isola, right?" she asks
me, and I nod.

"Right, well, Isola, this is history of Dragca.
You're lucky that we just started learning the history
of the royal family," she grins, "I'm sure you will
pass this class easily," she winks.

"Sure, the *princess* will get everything right," a
guy near the front says sarcastically. He has light-red
hair, and his brown eyes glare at me before turning
back to the teacher.

"Just for that comment, you can hand out the
books, Rye," the teacher snaps at him, and he slides
out of his seat and grabs a few books.

"For Isola's benefit, I will introduce myself, I am
Miss Claire," the teacher starts off, picking up a
whiteboard pen, and walking over to the whiteboard.
Rye drops a book on my desk, still glaring at me,
before he walks back to his seat.

"Can anyone tell me the name of the very first
king of Dragca?" she asks, looking at me, but I don't
have a clue. I probably should have read some of the
books my father left with us on Earth, like Jace did. A
sharp pain lances through me as I picture him, sitting

on my bed, reading the books. I remember him laughing when I said I didn't want to know anything about some old dead people. Looking back, I was innocent and stupid, I should have listened to Jace.

"Icahn Dragice was the first king; he took the throne after the war of fire and ice. Many ice dragons were killed, as well as fire dragons, but it was Icahn who created peace," a girl two desks in front of me says.

"Very good. Yes, Icahn Dragice was the only one of his family that wanted peace, and he was awarded the throne because of his actions. Up until then, a fight to the death between siblings was the only way to win the throne. Please open your books to page fifty-one," Miss Claire says as she starts writing on the board. I flip my book open to the page she wanted, and there are three paragraphs and a drawing of a large blue dragon, covered in ice. I don't know if that's what I look like when I shift, but I remember Jace's dragon, and he was a little smaller than the one in this drawing.

"As we all know, there are two different forms of dragons, ice and fire. Ice dragons have kept the throne for many years because fire dragons have a natural weakness to ice. If we are in contact with dragon ice for too long, it can kill us," she says with a pointed look over at Rye. "Maybe some of you should remember that before annoying the only ice dragon here," she adds, making me chuckle and like her instantly. A few students give me a nervous look, and the whispering starts up again.

"Now, read your book, pages 51 to 91 please. I'm going to test you on it in an hour," she comments, and I start reading. The first page is mainly full of information on Icahn; how he grew up and that his cousins were the ones that started the war. When they were killed, Icahn was the next in line, but the war meant no one was on the fire throne at the time. I turn the page over, and there's a drawing. It is a depiction of Icahn, holding a staff, with an orb on the top and a dragon curled around it. He has long white hair, braided at the sides, and he is huge, built like a giant. I read the next few pages, but no one talks about the staff, and I flip back, staring down at it. Maybe it's just my dragon side and her fascination with collecting shiny things, but I can't stop staring. I skip to the end of the book, hoping to find an index, but instead, there's another passage that I read in shock.

Icahn's first wife was known to be beautiful, but many never realised that it was her strength that made Icahn love her. During a fight on the battlefield, a dragon guard ran away when he was needed most, leaving Icahn alone to fight many fire dragons. Icahn was on the verge of defeat when his wife threw herself in front of him, taking a sword through the heart as she killed the other dragons with her ice. Her last words are the curse on the dragon guard, the curse that was sealed with royal blood.

I turn the page to find the curse written in fancy writing on its own, little fire and ice dragons painted at the sides around it.

"I curse the dragon guard and all its blood, to die for the royal throne and whoever sits upon it.
To desert the throne is to be killed. Either by fate or the throne.
One day, the curse will break due to the final promise.
If a dragon guard ever falls for a royal dragon, then they will lose their dragon in return.
This curse is final and unbreakable on my death.
The dragon guard will pay, and the curse will collect.
Ice will rule, and the dragon guard will protect."

I STOP READING when Miss Claire claps and begins talking, but I think over and over about the curse, a horrible curse, all because one dragon guard ran in a war. A curse that my father uses to control his dragon guard army, and ensure they do everything he demands. No wonder they hate us, the royals who control them but can never set them free. We can't even love them, nor can they love us, or the price would be their dragons. *A fate worse than death.*

CHAPTER
SIX
ISOLA

"How was your first class?" Thorne asks as I walk to him after leaving history. I slide the two textbooks under my arms before I answer.

"Good and bad," I say, thinking that I liked the teacher, but when she said I have to study all these books to catch up the two months I'm behind, that wasn't so great. I love reading, but not this kind of reading. One book is just about the farming lands and what we grow. I need to know every type of edible plant, as well as the unusable ones, grown in Dragca in time for a test in a month.

"Here, hand me those," he says, and I laugh a little.

"Just because I'm a girl, doesn't mean I need a

man to hold stuff for me. I can carry them, Thorne, but thanks," I say, squeezing around a couple of students to look at the locker numbers. I'm at eighty, so I keep walking until I find mine. Opening it up, I slide all my books in before slamming it shut again. I will have to remember to get them out, but I'm not carrying them around all day.

"What's next?" I ask Thorne.

"Lunch, and then two hours in geometry," he says and points down the stairs. *Food*. Food sounds better than it did a few hours ago.

"So how did you get here? Land a job as the dragon guard escorting me around?" I ask Thorne as I expected an older guard. Admittedly though, I don't know much about dragon guards.

"My family is close to the throne, so they thought it would be smart to have me near you. I've also passed a lot of assignments," he tells me as we get down the stairs and follow the students walking down the corridor by the door.

"Assignments?" I ask him.

"We are given tasks to train us, both here and on Earth. You may be born a dragon guard and live to the curse's rules, but it doesn't mean you instantly become a good fighter," he tells me and holds a door open for me. I walk into the large lunch room that has circle tables and what looks like a buffet towards the front, with a kitchen behind it. The tables are mostly full, and it's noisy as dragons walk around, everyone giving me hostile looks.

"Help yourself, I'm just going to check on something. I won't be far from you," he tells me and walks out of the room before I can reply to him. I turn away and walk across to the buffet. I am picking up a tray when someone bumps into me.

"Watch it," a deep voice snaps, and I turn to see Dagan Fire staring down at me. His eyes are slightly black on the edges, but they quickly snap back to a deep-blue colour.

"Oh, it's the moody guard," I reply blankly, and turn back around.

"Is that the princess?" I hear another male voice ask, and I turn to see a guy about our age watching me. He has a short, tidy black beard, curly black hair and tanned skin. He is dressed in the all-leather uniform, and I can see two swords crossed on his back. His green eyes watch me curiously, just as I watch him. *What is with this place and all the dragons being hot?* Even thinking of any of them as attractive sends waves of pain through me, and my own dragon stirs in my mind as I picture Jace. I quickly turn around when I realize I've been staring at them for way too long. *God, everyone is going to think I'm mad.*

"I told you, Korbin, she is as crazy as they come," Dagan says, chuckling. I take a deep breath, trying not to react to the idiots.

"And stunning, you said she was stunning," Korbin replies, his voice low and deep.

"Well, she is stunning, but the crazy ones always are," Dagan replies, and I slam my tray down on the side before turning to face them.

"I am standing right here, don't talk about me like I'm not," I snap as they both look at me, and then at each other, before they start laughing.

"Little princess, you don't have the throne yet, and I won't listen to a word you say. So, if I want to talk about you, I will," Korbin finally says with a shrug. *You know, after they both stop laughing.*

"She won't inherit the throne anyway, not since her precious little prince was killed," Dagan says, "Such a shame about that," he tuts. I lock my eyes with him as anger flows through me, both me and my dragon. I let my dragon out, feeling my eyes glaze over as my hands start to freeze everything near us. Dagan and Korbin take a step back as snow begins to fall from my hands, and I don't move as I try to calm myself down.

"Kill them?" my dragon whispers in my mind; her sadness and anger are overwhelming and make me take a deep gasp. Unfortunately, she uses that as an opportunity to completely take over, shooting ice out of my hands in giant waves, and then spreading across the floor as I fall. I don't hear or see a thing as my dragon pushes against my mind, trying to make me shift and allow her to act on her anger. Her pain is clouding her judgement, making her view everything as a threat and want to destroy all she sees.

"Listen to me, dragon, this is not the way. They didn't hurt Jace, and you could kill them," I manage to grind out in my head, begging her to listen. She doesn't stop, but she lets me speak to her, lowering the barrier between us a tad.

"We need to work together to get revenge on the real dragon that did this to us, that hurt Jace. Killing these guards won't do that," I beg her, feeling my arms warm up and bones begin to move as the shift starts to happen.

"Please, no," I beg her once more, and she whines in my head, a whine that transforms into a roar that fills my ears as she pulls back.

"Revenge, we have to get revenge," she whispers to me, and for the first time in years, we are in complete agreement. I blink my eyes open, looking

63

up at icicles hanging from the ceiling. My breath comes out in cold white puffs as I struggle to sit up. All around me is a thick wall of ice; I can't see anything, and no one can get to me. I lift myself up, trying not to slip on the ice on the floor as I walk to the ice wall and place my hand on it. I punch my hand through the ice, cutting my knuckles a little. I punch a hole next to it and then another one, until there's a big enough gap for me to climb through. The sight in front of me causes me to forget the cuts stinging my knuckles as I stop and stare in shock. All the students are frozen; the whole room looks like they tried to run away from me, but didn't get far. *Dragon ice can kill fire dragons if they are exposed to it for too long, shit.* I run over to Dagan and Korbin, who are frozen in place with their eyes completely black, as if they tried to call their dragons before this happened.

"*Naughty princess,* tut, tut," I hear a deep, throaty voice say, and I move around Dagan to see Elias Fire walking towards me, burning footsteps in the ice as he goes. He has a leather jacket on and a cigarette in his hand which he drops on the floor, crushing it with his boot.

"I didn't mean to–" I start to try and explain, and he grins at me, lifts his hand and places a finger against his lips. I step back as he swings his arms out, and fire shoots out of them in the shape of a dragon as he stands still. He burns away the ice, never harming the fireproof students, who fall off their chairs or collapse to the ground. The doors bang open behind Elias, just as his fire passes them, and there my uncle stands. He has a strained expression on his face, and his hands firmly planted on his hips.

"My office, now," my uncle demands as he walks further into the room with Thorne at his side, and watches Elias put the rest of the fire out. Dagan falls to the ground when he is free of the ice, with Korbin following moments later.

"This is your fault," Dagan snaps, glaring up at me.

"Dagan, Korbin, Elias, Thorne, and Isola, get to my office. Everyone else to the medical bay to be checked over," my uncle shouts as Elias lowers his hands. I look around at the students on the floor, wiping ice off of themselves and struggling to stand up. The hostile glares they gave me when I first walked in here are replaced with pure hate now. *Best first day ever.*

"Such a naughty little *princess*, aren't you?" Elias taunts with a low chuckle, before turning and walking straight back out.

CHAPTER
SEVEN

ISOLA

"**Y**ou froze the entire room! A goddamn room full of fire dragons . . . who you nearly killed, Isola!" my uncle shouts, while I look down at the floor. It was an accident, but I doubt telling him that will make a difference at the moment. He has been shouting at me for the last twenty minutes, and nothing I've tried to say has made even a little difference. If anything, my trying to speak a word just annoys him more.

"All because I called you stunning," Dagan says in a cocky tone, speaking for the first time. Both my uncle and I turn to glare at him. That was not all that he said, and the ass knows it. He holds his hands up, "Well, you are."

"Congratulations, Dagan, you and your friends

have a new job. You are not leaving this school for the rest of the year," my uncle says clapping. "You can forget that assignment in Florida."

"What new job?" Korbin asks, moving away from the door he was silently leaning against.

"Watching my niece, the goddamn princess, who is meant to be able to control her powers," he stops to glare at me again before continuing his rant, "and making sure she doesn't freeze everyone . . . again."

"No," Korbin says firmly, making my uncle laugh coldly. I look over to see Elias and Thorne just staring at me, one of them on each side of the room, and neither are listening to my uncle.

"Also, if I catch one of you calling her stunning, flirting, or breaking any of the rules, I will personally kick you out, and none of you will stay in Dragca. I don't give a damn who you think you are," he tells the four most dangerous dragons in this school. You don't tell the royal guards' what to do unless you're the king. The royal guards only protect my family because they are cursed to do so. *Until we are all dead that is.* It doesn't mean they would be punished for killing my uncle as he isn't a royal, so I'm surprised he just told them what to do.

"Hell, no," Dagan chuckles, which dies away when he looks at my uncle.

"Now, get out," my uncle commands, a dark-sounding threat lacing his words, and to my surprise, the guys walk out without a word. I go to follow them, but my uncle stops me.

"Isola, you will stay. Shut the door behind them," he says. I shut the door, but not before I see Dagan pulling Elias away from Thorne. They are both glaring at each other with anger in their eyes, and look close to fighting. *What the hell is that about?*

"You will need constant supervision now, and I am trusting you to get your powers under control. We need you to be strong, not out of control," he says, and gets up, walking to the window. "Every Sunday morning, you will fly to the mountains with Dagan and Korbin and train with them, because they are the best fighters we have. Every Saturday, you will spend all day with me, and I will teach you valuable lessons. Thorne can teach you the history of Dragca after classes on Friday, your least busy day of the week. I trust him, and he is smartest of them all in history anyway," he tells me.

"And Elias?" I ask.

"Is too out of control to be trusted to train or teach you anything. He will protect you, as he is a dragon guard, but I don't trust him alone with you. I wish for you to stay away from Elias, unless you need him to save you from danger," he says, growling slightly.

"Fine," I say, wondering what exactly Elias has done to make my uncle trust him so little. Also, I'm hating the small part of me that wants to spend time with Elias, just because my uncle told me not to. *Like he is forbidden fruit or something.*

"I hope I don't have to remind you that relationships between the royal family and the dragon guard is a death sentence for you both. The curse–" he starts, and I cut him off.

"I know about the curse, I read it this morning," I tell him.

"Good, then you understand why it is so very important that you stay away from them, and keep your relationship strictly business. Think of them as bodyguards, nothing more," he tells me. I don't say anything as the words run around my mind, this is why my family has never mixed with fire dragons, because of the risk of this curse.

"I still love Jace," I admit.

"The dead do not need your love," he states, almost gently but still strict with every word like I'm coming to expect from him.

"But, he has it, and my vow of revenge," I say, and he bows his head to me.

G. BAILEY

"Revenge is a much better feeling than love. As you already know, love is a weakness to us. Revenge is a strength, it gives you determination, a reason to fight," he comments.

"Love is not a weakness," I argue, and he laughs, looking back at the window.

"It is the weakness of every dragon and human alike. Every species known to us that can love is weak because of it. Love makes you weak, and you are proof of that. You are weak because of Jacian's death," he says.

"That's not true, I am not weak," I insist, my dragon backing me in my mind.

"You are, and you being weak makes the whole of Dragca weak," he scolds me as I cross my arms and glare at him.

"Focus on revenge, Isola, not other feelings," he tells me firmly before I can reply to him. I walk to the door, looking back at my uncle as I rest a hand on the door handle.

"Who did you lose?" I ask, hearing the pain of his loss behind his angry words. No one is that angry without losing someone close.

"Everyone I've ever loved is dead, every person I consider family. Now, leave," he demands. His voice is so detached that I don't how to reply to him.

70

Instead, I choose to just open the door and walk out. Thorne is leaning against the wall, his hands in his pockets, and his hazel eyes look up at me.

"Interesting first day, Issy," he says, walking over, and stopping right in front of me.

"Only attempted to kill my whole class, got myself extra training, and I bet I made a whole lot of enemies here," I shrug, making him laugh. I feel my lips turn up in a smile before I end up laughing with him.

"Classes have been cancelled for the day and–" he stops when he sees my hands, and he picks them up.

"How did you do this?" he asks, looking at my blood-covered knuckles, and I flinch when he rubs a finger over one of the cuts. I had actually forgotten about them.

"I had to break through the wall of ice I made, well, that my dragon made when she got mad," I respond automatically. I see the realization float across Thorne's face at what my words mean. My ice can hurt me, and my dragon healing doesn't work to fix the cuts. It's a well-kept secret of ice dragons, not many people know it and for good reason.

"I don't know much about ice dragons or anything, but come back to my room, so I can clean

71

that up. I can stitch a few places up to stop the bleeding," he says gently as he lets go of my hands.

"Alright," I say, knowing I can't go to my uncle for help, and I don't want anyone else knowing how vulnerable I am to my own powers. Thorne walks close to my side, our arms brushing as we walk up the stairs, and past my bedroom. We walk past the others until we get to another staircase. This staircase leads all the way up to the top of the tower, and you can see all the way up, and see the hundreds of rooms lining the tower.

"All the guards staying at Dragca Academy live in these rooms," he tells me as we start to climb. We pass two doors on the walk up before he stops and gets a key out of his cloak. He opens his door and waves me in. Thorne's room is like mine in size, but he has a tiny window and a small bed with blue sheets. There is a pile of books on his bedside cabinet, with one still open. I walk over and see it open to a page on the history of ice dragons.

"Sit, I have a first aid box in the bathroom," Thorne instructs as he shuts the door and undoes his cloak, hanging it over the bathroom door. I keep my eyes on the way the tight leather is stretched across his muscular frame, showing off his toned stomach and chest. When I look up, he is watching me as he sifts through a cabinet above the sink, but he quickly glances away. I shake my head, reminding myself that he is just helping me, and it doesn't matter how damn hot he is.

"What happened in the lunch room?" he asks, as he comes and kneels in front of me. I watch as he opens the box, pulling out everything he needs and laying it out on the floor. He gets some alcohol and pours it on a cloth, before he grabs my right hand. He starts cleaning it as I bite down on my lip from the stinging pain.

"If I answer that, can I ask you something?" I bargain. He looks at me, and nods once before focusing on my hands again. He wraps the knuckles, clearly deciding they don't need any stitches before taking my left hand, which is the far worse of the two.

"Dagan and Korbin, they said something about Jace . . . I lost control," I say, not being able to look at Thorne as I speak.

"Understandable, it hasn't been long since you lost him," Thorne says gently. When he tilts his head to the side, I see a smudge of what looks like brown paint on his neck.

"Do you paint?" I ask, pointing at it, and he quickly rubs it away.

"No," he says, his voice colder than before.

"Why do you hate Elias?" I ask, watching how he completely tenses up and squeezes my hand a little tighter.

"He killed someone close to me," he says, his tone gruff as he reaches into the box and gets some butterfly stitches out, sorting my left hand before wrapping it up.

"I'm sorry, who was it?" I ask.

"I don't owe you another answer, Isola," he snaps, the iciness of his tone makes me pull my hands away from him. I stand up, walking around him, pausing as I open the door.

"No, you owe me nothing, but I am sorry. I know what it's like to have the people you love murdered when there is nothing you can do to stop it," I tell him. I quickly walk out of the room before I do something stupid, like let him see me cry.

EIGHT

ISOLA

"Wake up," a voice shouts, and then there's loud banging on my door. I roll over and groan into my pillow as I rub my tired eyes. I look over at the gap in the curtains, only to see that it's still dark out. Sliding myself out of bed, I move to shout at whoever is stupid enough to wake me up this early. *It's inhuman, that's what it is; no one should be awake before the sun rises.* I walk over to the door, pulling it open and glaring at Korbin who is jogging on the spot outside my room. He has a short vest on, showing off white tattoos that trail up his arms and disappear into the vest.

"Eyes up, doll," Korbin says, laughing when I glare at him and rub my eyes.

"I'm half asleep, and this *doll* is not fucking impressed, what the hell do you want?" I snap, making him laugh louder.

"I like you already, but we have a two-mile run to do. So, *doll*, get some running gear on as we only have two hours before class," he says, making my jaw drop open.

"I don't run, not unless something is chasing me, and even then, I'd rather take my chances with it," I grumble. He steps closer to me, before leaning down to growl into my ear.

"You can get your butt in there and get changed for our run, or I can throw you over my shoulder, take you to the woods, and throw fireballs at your ass to make you run," he warns me.

"Seems like you're focused on my ass a lot in that sentence," I respond, making him grin at me.

"Get changed, flirting with me won't make me be any nicer to you," he says, moving back and starting to do that annoying jogging thing again. *Why is he so happy, and more importantly, awake at this time in the morning?*

"I wasn't–" I snap, and he interrupts me.

"Get changed."

"So bossy," I groan, giving up because I'm pretty sure he would throw fireballs at me and enjoy it. *I'm*

76

also pretty sure I wouldn't. I turn around and walk back into my room, slamming the door shut behind me. I quickly dive through my suitcase to try to find my active-wear. I really need to unpack. Finding what I need, I pull the yoga top, leggings, and small jacket on.

"Hurry up," Korbin shouts, banging on the door once. I resist the urge to throw my trainers at the door, deciding to put them on, and pull my hair up into a ponytail instead. I brush my teeth, then throw some water on my face before walking out of the room.

"About time," Korbin begins before pausing. His eyes trail over me, starting at my feet and making their way up my body slowly, as he rubs his beard with one hand.

"Is this what humans wear? Tight, bright clothes?" he questions, and I look down at my bright-pink leggings and black crop top.

"Some people live in clothes like this, but never actually work out in them. They are designed for working out," I shrug, so used to seeing humans wearing them that I never considered that it would be weird at all.

"Humans are strange," he states before turning and running down the stairs. I start after him, but he goes so fast that he is standing leaning against the wall when I finally reach the bottom. He smiles arrogantly, before taking off and running out of the room. We run straight down the corridor to the entrance hall, where he holds the door open for me.

"So, where are we running?" I ask.

"In the forest. Don't worry, it's protected, and Dagan is out flying in dragon form, keeping an eye out," he says, just as a loud roar shakes the trees.

"Well, he is closer than I thought," Korbin laughs, before running straight towards the trees. I run after him, getting to his side as we get to the path in the woods. He keeps at a steady pace as I take the opportunity to look around. The path is smooth, and there are little hills at the side that drop down into more trees. I look up at the sunrise, seeing the pinks and purples spreading across the sky around the two suns. The large green trees stretch so high that they almost look like they are touching the sky, it's amazing. I have to look down and focus on my breathing when running gets harder, making me realize how out of shape I am. *I seriously don't run.*

"How much longer?" I ask as the trees all start to look the same. I stop, breathing heavily as I put my hands on my knees.

"The path takes an hour and a half to run at this

speed, and we have been running for twenty minutes," he says plainly.

"Oh my god," I pant out. "It felt like forever, I'm done," I state, making him chuckle, and I look up.

"We have an hour left. Don't make me get the fireballs started," he threatens, and I just glare at him.

"I'm not going to do this every day. What is the point?" I ask as I get my breath back and lean against a nearby tree. Korbin sighs, holding his hand in the air and making a small fireball.

"Now, doll, I wasn't kidding about throwing fireballs at your ass if you don't start running. I'm not paid to explain anything to you," he says, making the fireball in his hand larger. I move away from the tree, walking straight up to him, and placing my hand into the fire. It warms my hand, but it doesn't hurt me one bit.

"Fire doesn't hurt me, so there would be no point, other than burning my clothes. Do you really want to see my ass that badly?" I ask, watching his eyes widen in shock. I lower my hand when he stops the fire and steps closer. I have to tilt my head up to meet his eyes as we both glare at each other.

"I think you're the one obsessed with your pretty little ass, not me. You keep bringing it up."

"I think you're in denial," I chuckle, and he narrows his eyes at me.

"Well, being *princess* and all, I guess you would be right about everything," he says, the amount of venom and sarcasm in his words makes me want to back away from him. I don't, I just end up staring into his green eyes. They are a dark-green with black around them, and in places, they have little tints of hazel. They are amazing, so deep and different from anyone else's I've seen.

"Why do you hate me?" I ask, seeing his dislike in his eyes.

"Do you have any clue what it is like to be a slave to the throne? Knowing that your only place in the world is to die for the royal family. That the curse will always ruin every part of your life, and knowing you can never really be free?" he asks me.

"Who says I'm free? There is no curse on the throne, but there is a burden that no one, particularly me, wants," I reply.

"But you *can* run, you can escape. Magic won't make you choose to allow the curse to kill you, or come back to a king that would kill you for deserting him," he spits out.

"He wouldn't do that," I shake my head as Korbin takes a step back and laughs.

"Tell my parents and sister that. Oh wait, you can't, because they are dead for wanting to be free," he growls at me. His vehemence makes me stumble back with a slight bit of fear, but then he turns away from me. I take a deep breath before stepping closer, feeling like I need to tell him something, anything that I can to make this better. I didn't know my father was like that, I didn't even know the words of the curse until yesterday. I place my hand on his shoulder, his skin burning hot under my touch.

"I'm sorry, I didn't know about my father, or even the specifics of the curse until recently. I would never do that to anyone."

"Then you should know not to touch me. I have to be nothing to you, not even a friend," he says, glancing over his shoulder and shrugging my hand off.

"I know that," I reply, feeling stupid for trying to comfort him.

"There's still a lot you do not know, doll," he states cryptically as he narrows his eyes at me and walks away. "Run or don't, but being in the best phys-ical shape you can makes your dragon stronger," he says, just before he runs off. I stand and watch for a second before taking off after him, and we don't say a word for the rest of the run.

CHAPTER
NINE

DAGAN

"What happened in there? Why did you tell her about your past? You know we can't be friends with her, we can't be anything to her," I ask Korbin as we watch Isola run towards the academy, dressed in the tightest bloody clothes I've ever seen. *What the hell is she wearing, and why does she look so fucking hot in it?*

"I don't know, she messes with my head when I'm near her, and I forget everything planned," he says with a groan, rubbing his face as he watches Isola, like I do, until we can't see her as she gets inside the academy.

"She can't mess with your head. Your parents–" I say.

"I know, I'm not an idiot," Korbin interrupts, looking over at me.

"I get it, she is attractive and damn innocent in all this. But, it has to stop, and she has to bear the price in the end. Being her friend–it's not part of our job, and is fucking dangerous," I say, making sure he is looking at me. "Don't get close."

"Who are you trying to kid? I've known you my whole life, and I know when you want something," Korbin says, making my dragon growl low.

"You don't know anything, just like you told her," I growl.

"I know something is up. You looked shocked to see her yesterday. Why?" he asks. I try to ignore how my dragon is thinking about her, how we watched her all the way around the woods, and I couldn't get my dragon to focus on anything but Isola. It's a total mind fuck when your dragon finds a treasure he wants, and you can't explain why we can't have her. It's more confusing when I can't stop thinking about her either.

"I remember meeting her, but I don't want to talk about it," I refuse to even think about it. I won't be thanking her for anything.

"Then keep your eyes off her," he warns.

"It's all my dragon," I growl, watching as Korbin's eyes turn slightly black.

"I get it," is all he says.

"What are we going to do about Thorne?" I ask, needing to discuss him. I don't know why he's here, he wasn't meant to be.

"Watch him, and hope he doesn't drop us all in it," Korbin says as I roll my lip ring between my lips, and look back at the castle.

"We should all take turns watching both him and Isola. We need Elias to actually help us and not fuck around while he is here," I mutter, knowing my brother can't be trusted to do anything that doesn't benefit himself.

"Talk of the devil," I mutter. My brother's dragon is diving out the sky and flying straight towards us. Elias' dragon is all black with red claws and a nasty temper, not far off from my brother's. He lands with a thump in front of us, roaring loudly before shifting, and my brother is left kneeling on the ground. He stands up, reaching inside his leather jacket and pulling out a cigarette. He lights it up before walking over to us.

"I heard my name," he says, blowing smoke at Korbin and smirking when he doesn't look impressed.

"Where have you been? You're meant to be watching Isola this morning," I question him.

"I'm here, aren't I?" he replies, shrugging a shoulder and looking back at the castle.

"She is inside, in the shower by the sounds of it," he says and smirks at me, "I wish I could join her," he taunts. His eyes turn black as his dragon says something that makes him grin around his cigarette.

"No fucking her, no messing around, or you will get kicked out of this place, just like you did when we went to school here," I warn him.

"Sleeping with three of the teachers was worth it," he shrugs.

"We need to be here, and you know why. If he finds out–" I stop talking when my brother's face goes serious.

"I'm going to fucking watch the *princess*," he snaps and turns around, walking towards the castle before I can say anything else to him.

"Do you trust him?" Korbin asks when Elias is out of sight.

"He's my brother, of course I do," I reply.

"And if he chooses the wrong side?" he asks.

"He won't, so it doesn't matter," I state. My brother may act like a complete asshole, but he knows the end goal of being here. We have a job to do, and nothing can mess with that job. It could mean the end of everything, and even my brother isn't stupid enough to mess that up.

"Your judgement is too clouded by the fact he is your brother. You don't see how out of control he is, and always has been," he replies.

"Don't Kor," I warn him, and he places his hand on my shoulder.

"I'm your friend, if I didn't say it, I would be lying to you," he says gently.

"Elias has never loved anyone, never given a shit. I don't care what some prophecy says. He won't fuck this up," I shrug his hand off and walk away. As I get closer, I pick up the sweet, icy scent of Isola.

"*Mine, she will be mine, and you will save her*," my dragon whispers to me. For the first time in years, I slam a barrier down between us before punching the wall near the door.

"For fuck's sake," I mutter. The third prophecy says one of the brothers will fall. Everyone thinks it is Elias, yet it's my dragon that already thinks of Isola as his. The third prophecy, the one that no one knows except for the king and us. Well, and the fire rebellion. The only one who can never know is Isola. It would destroy her—and us.

CHAPTER
TEN
ISOLA

"How was your run?" Thorne immediately asks when I answer the door. He asks nicely, no sign of the ire from our talk last night. I decide to not mention it and forget he acted weird as I walk out of my room.

"Good but painful, what classes do I have today? Please tell me it's nothing physical," I groan.

"It's Herbololgy, and I'm escorting the princess today," I hear said behind me, and I turn to see Elias leaning against the wall of the stairs just above me.

"I have to stay with Isola at all times, you are not needed," Thorne sneers. He places a hand on my waist and stares up at Elias, who just seems focused on Thorne's hand.

"Guys, we are going to be late. You can argue,

fight, or measure each other's dicks to see which is bigger later. I need a guide to class," I say, stepping away from Thorne as he coughs on a laugh, and I see Elias smirk.

"Mine's bigger, I'm sure, but let's go," Elias says, and jumps over the bars of the staircase. I look down to see him land perfectly on the floor below.

"Cocky asshole," Thorne mutters, walking down the corridor, and I quickly follow. When I get to the bottom of the stairs, the guys are just staring at each other. Both of their eyes are turning black, and Thorne even has fire sparks falling from his fingers.

"Guys?" I ask, trying to get their attention. They both ignore me, and I just give up. Clearly those two can't work together.

"Why are you even here, Elias? Don't you have work for the king to do? Innocent families to kill?" Thorne asks snidely. Elias steps closer, pulling up his fist and slamming it into Thorne's face. Thorne crashes into the wall, shaking the tower before standing up.

"Don't you like the truth, or do you not like the princess knowing what you really are?" he asks.

"Don't bring me into this, I barely know either of you," I say, holding my hands up. They continue to ignore me. I might as well just walk away, but I'm scared they might actually try to kill each other, and bring the castle down in the process.

"I don't care what she knows or thinks," Elias says loudly, and then lowers his voice, "but your family wasn't innocent. You need to get the fuck over it because you know what they did." Thorne stares at him, not replying. Elias walks past me in the doorway and down the corridor.

"Come on, my naughty princess, you're going to be late for class," Elias calls. I look back to see Thorne looking at the ground, his arms burning with fire, but he doesn't say a word.

"Go," Thorne says so quietly that if I wasn't a dragon, I wouldn't have heard it. I run to catch up with Elias, stopping at his side as we walk down the corridors, mixing in with the students going to class.

"You must think I'm a monster, eh?" Elias asks me, after a few moments of awkward silence.

"Are you?" I question.

"We are all monsters, I think. It's inside of us," he says.

"I don't think you're a monster, perhaps just damaged and broken. Maybe working for the wrong side, I don't know. I'm not going to judge you, especially not on something I don't fully know the details of," I comment.

"Like you," he chuckles and stops walking. Elias moves close enough that I'm overwhelmed by his scent. It's a smoky musk, like a bonfire on a cold night, and I can't help but want to be closer.

"What?" I end up asking like an idiot, forgetting what we were even talking about.

"Broken in here," he steps closer and places his hand on my heart. Reaching forward with his other hand, he pushes a bit of my hair behind my ear as I suck in a ragged breath. I end up just staring at him, lost in his eyes. Those light-blue eyes are so much like Dagan's, but Elias has a black ring around his pupil. Both are seriously stunning to look at.

"You are so, so dangerous for someone like me, princess," he murmurs, stepping back, and nodding his head at the door like nothing just happened.

"Your class is in there. I'm not listening to that shit about plants again, so I will be out here," he says. I nod, speechless, walking to the door and opening it up, rather than replying to him. I feel his eyes on me, and it makes me look back, and Elias smirks before lightly chuckling.

"What's funny?" I ask. He doesn't reply to me, only pulling out a cigarette and lighting it up with his finger.

"Nothing you want to know, my naughty

princess," he grins. Shaking my head, I open the door further and walk in.

"Miss Dragice, we have been waiting," the male voice says as I walk into a room covered in plants. It's a bit of a surprise in here, considering that you can't see the walls or floors from the amount of plants and trees in here. Actually, I don't even think there is a floor when I look down to see grass beneath my boots. I walk around a bush near the door to get to an old man standing in the middle of five students. He has a weird, green top hat on, a matching suit and holds a walking stick, which he taps on the floor.

"Come on, come on, we don't have much time today. I am Mr. Oneen," he urges. I move closer, standing next to a girl who glares at me as she pushes her strawberry-blonde hair over her shoulder before moving away. I've never had a girl as friend, with human girls hating me from the moment they saw me. It seems nothing is different here, except for the reasons why they hate me. I wonder if she, or any of the others, were in the cafeteria yesterday. It would make sense of all the hate-filled glares I'm receiving. I doubt it would make them feel better to know it was by accident that I nearly killed them.

"Welcome to Herbology. As you know, we live in a magical world full of unusual and rare plants. We also have rare creatures that roam the forest, but that is something you will learn about in wildlife class with me later in the week," he says as he smiles at me. "No, this class is about the plants, trees, flowers, and even the grass you walk on. It is about how magic is woven into this world and how the plant life can help us, like we can help them," he tells everyone before walking over to a plant pot and bringing it over.

"Come and see," he waves us closer, and we all gather around as he puts the pot on the ground. In the soil, there is only a tiny plant with light-green leaves.

"Watch this," Mr. Oneen chuckles at our confused faces before he starts to whistle. We watch as the plant shakes, and then starts growing as Mr. Oneen whistles more loudly, occasionally changing pitch. The plant continues to get bigger, and branches stretch out, with little purple shells hanging from them. Mr. Oneen stops when the tree touches the ceiling, surrounding us with its branches that hang low. I watch as he breaks one of the purple shells off the tree and comes back to the middle of the circle. He goes to open it and then seems to realize we are all still standing here. He waves one hand in the air.

"Will you all please get one, and open it for me," he asks. I reach for the nearest shell, pulling it off of the branch, and picking open the tough shell. Inside is a small purple round-shaped object.

"As Isola knows, humans have 'sweets' which are copied off the idea of these trees," he says and pops his purple sweet into his mouth, crunching it around. "These sweets have healing properties, say if your dragon throws too much fire," he pauses to smile at me, "or ice, this will heal your sore throat. "In this class, I will teach you about the magic of the plants around you," he says as he places a hand on the tree. "The magic of the plants, the forests, and even the mountains are what protect our world from the human world. They even look after us by making natural healing elements for dragons," he says as he steps away and places both of his hands on his walking stick.

"Please go around the room, find a plant of your choice, and take it back to your room," he instructs, but none of us move.

"What do we do with the plant, sir?" I ask when no one else seems inclined to speak up, and he laughs.

"Oh, I forgot to mention that. I want you to study the plant, tell me what it does, and how it can be used. You will pass the class if you can figure it out," he waves a hand around the room. "Go."

I walk out of the cluster of branches, away from

the other students and down the rows of potted plants of different sizes and colours. I stop when I see an ice-blue plant. It's tiny, with only two leaves in a black pot filled with soil. I pick it up, walking back to the teacher, who looks down at the plant.

"Perfect," he nods his head, gently stroking the plant.

"Perfect for an ice dragon, I guess," I smile at him. He nods, a surprised look on his face, as he looks at me once more and then back to the plant.

"Did you know—your mother chose the exact same plant," he tells me, shocking me.

"No," I say quietly.

"There is something about the BlueTay plant that calls to ice dragons I believe," he smiles. "You may leave now, and take it back to your room," he says and walks away to help another student before I can ask him anything else.

ELEVEN

"Isola?" Thorne's voice shouts after the door is knocked on three times. I run over, pulling it open, and he is standing with three books in his hands, then his head tilts to the side.

"Are you going to let me in?" he asks, almost cheekily.

"Are they for me?" I ask, as he walks past me into my room and drops them onto my bed.

"Well, sort of, I'm going to teach you tonight. Remember?" he asks, and I remember what my uncle said about him teaching me something. *There goes my plan to sleep for the rest of the afternoon.*

"What exactly are you going to teach me about?" I ask, scrunching my face up at the idea of studying all night.

"Politics," he says and smiles at my pulled face.

"Really? That's what you have to teach me?" I ask, groaning.

"Yes, really. You want to rule, yet have no idea of the councils and five selected that rule the five parts of Dragca," he states simply.

"I've never even heard of them," I say honestly, and he shakes his head, opening one of the books and sitting on the rug on the floor. I go and sit next to him, leaning over to see the picture-less book written in another language.

"It's written in Latin, but I will read it to you," he says.

"You can speak Latin?" I ask, watching as his hazel eyes turn to lock with mine.

"And French," he says, leaning a little closer and picking up a piece of my hair, twirling it with one of his fingers.

"Tes yeux sont comme de beaux trésors," he says softly as he lets my hair fall onto my chest.

"What does that mean?" I ask, and he looks away breaking that contact between us.

"Just that your eyes are bright," he says, but I have a feeling he is lying to me, not that I can prove it.

"Okay, so what are the five selected?" I ask, changing the subject onto what we should be doing.

"So, you know each major town, all five of them in Dragca have councils. In each council, there are four members, and they vote for one of them to become the selected. The selected has the final say, more power, and speaks directly to the king with any issues," he explains.

"That makes sense," I nod.

"Here it explains that the council have open meetings every Friday, where anyone with an issue can come and speak," he pauses for a second. "I went to one once," he tells me.

"What did you go for?" I ask.

"I went to get justice for my adoptive parents, against Elias," he tells me, his anger looks like it is almost vibrating through him until I move closer and rest my hand over his. He doesn't move, but he doesn't move his hand away from mine. I know I shouldn't comfort him, he is a dragon guard, yet here I am. *I never said I was smart.*

"You don't have to tell me if you don't want to," I say, and he leans back, putting the book down on the floor with his free hand.

"I might as well tell you before Elias tells you the twisted version," he says, and I stay quiet. I don't think Elias would bother making up any excuses, he seems like the type to own the deaths he has caused. The dragon guards do kill, and I'm sure Thorne has killed to get to where he is now.

"My adoptive parents, my father to be exact, helped his brother to kill someone very important, but he was made to do it," he shakes his head.

"Who?" I ask, wondering who his uncle killed, and why his father would be killed for helping.

"It doesn't matter, what matters is that he shouldn't have been made to help, and Elias was ordered to find him and kill him for it. My mother killed herself because of the loss of her mate two days after his death,"

"I'm so sorry," I say, and he looks over at me.

"So am I. I wanted to save them, but I couldn't. I hated feeling weak."

"I felt that way when I saw my mother dead, when I saw Jace dead. I'm never there to help them, always late," I whisper and he nods.

"How old were you?" I ask.

"It was two years ago that he was killed. I was training and didn't know they had been found. They had been on the run for years," he explains.

"Can you help me with something else?" I ask him after a lot of silence has passed between us.

"Sure," he smiles sadly.

"I have this plant, and I wondered if you could take me to the library, so I could find some books on it?" I ask.

"Yeah, let's go now, I'm not in the mood for studying," he says, jumping up and holding a hand out for me. He pulls me up before walking to the door and opening it for me. We walk down the quiet corridors, only passing a few students the whole time. The library is right at the end of the longest corridor in the castle, and it has big dark-wooden doors.

"This is the library, I can wait outside for you if you want," he offers, and I nod, walking a little away from him before stopping and walking back. I gently wrap my arms around his frozen body, hugging him and walking away before I look back at his reaction.

"What are you reading?" Elias asks, jumping onto the sofa next to me in the library and ruining my perfect silence. The library is even better than Thorne said it was, and I will have to remember to thank him later for bringing me here. It's the perfect mix between human technology and the ancient magic of Dragca. They even have chargers in here for Kindles, and modern books that the librarian told me they import from Earth every month. *I swear I'm never leaving this place.*

"Nothing," I quickly try to shut the book, but he easily takes it off me. I cover my face with my hands as he starts reading it out loud.

"His hands slide down my body, as his mouth

devours my own. I can't help the moan that escapes my lips when Enzo-" Elias begins reading louder. I jump over to his side of the sofa, slapping my hand over his mouth, and he laughs. I pull my book away, sliding it on the side as Elias keeps laughing.

"You really are a naughty princess, aren't you?" he asks me with a smirk. I roll my eyes at him before getting up and walking away. I hear him follow me as I walk down the aisles full of books, both modern and old mixed together in their respective categories. I get to the charging table, and picking up my Kindle, see that it's fully charged. I unplug it, practically giddy at the thought of logging myself in and finishing my book.

I take one more look at the massive library, the rows of bookshelves, the big windows, and pause to appreciate the old-fashioned, cozy feel to the place. I love it, it reminds me of the library from *Beauty and the Beast*. I keep walking when I hear Elias behind me, hoping to get back to my room before he comments on anything he just read.

"I'm only winding you up; it's cool that you read. Though, I had you down as a classic kind of girl, not the girly porn type," he says as he jumps out from behind a bookshelf and blocks my way out of the library. I find every word out his stupidly attractive mouth downright insulting to females. We should be allowed to read whatever we like, without being told it's porn.

"It's not girly porn," I stop walking and face him, as he laughs at me.

"Yes, it is. Books like that are written to get bored girls all hot and bothered," he says, stepping closer to me. I swallow when his rich, smoky smell hits me, and my dragon basically purrs in my mind.

"Don't even think about it," I tell her, watching as Elias tilts his head to the side.

"Mine," she replies simply. It's not a demand exactly, but it sounds like she has made her mind up on something she is keeping. She never said that about Jace; well, honestly, she only tolerated him, and I never really knew why. But he was still family in her mind, and she misses him as much as I do. Yet this damaged, kind of crazy and dangerous dragon, she wants to keep? *You have got to be kidding me.*

"I've never seen an ice dragon's eyes before," he says into the silence, only the sound of pages turning and the librarian falling asleep at the desk can be heard in the room.

"They're normal for me, but I couldn't remember fire dragon eyes, not until I saw them here," I comment.

"What *do* you remember from when you lived here?" he asks me, leaning back on the bookshelf.

"Why do you want to know?" I ask him in return, and he only smirks.

"I heard that before the queen was killed, there was peace in Dragca. I was too young when she died to remember that time, and I lived out in a poor village. I'm curious what the royals and the rich called peace," he states. I don't know that I really remember much to tell him.

"I remember big parties, long dresses, and beautiful dragons. I remember how my mother would travel to villages and give the people food," I say, thinking of how I remember my mother looking. She always had her long, white-blonde hair up in a bun, with two plaits on the sides and little curls that escaped. She always wore white or blue, never any other colors, and she smelled like sweets. I miss her so much. Honestly, I miss more of the dead than I love any of the living.

"You used to go with your mother," he tells me.

"Once, I went once with my mother, but she hid me. No one knew I went, how did you?" I ask, curious about how he could ever know that.

"Don't you remember? You gave me and Dagan

food and your gold rings," he says, making a flash-back pop into my mind.

"DON'T GO FAR," my mother warns me, her hands full and unable to grab on to me. She holds two baskets of food, and several guards with her also carry as much food as possible. I slip out two rolls of bread from the carriage and smile at her.

"I promise," I say cheekily, almost tripping on the deep mud on the ground that sticks to my white dress. I walk around the fountain, stopping when I see two boys my age sitting on the edge. One of them is drinking the water, and the other is staring at the ground, his black hair hiding his face.

"Hello," I say as I walk up to them, and they both turn to look at me. They are brothers, and are kind of cute, even as their dragons take over, making their eyes go black. I watch as they look at the bread in my hands.

"Here," I offer the bread to them, and they both shake their heads.

"Well, I'm just going to leave this here then," I say, placing it on the side of the fountain and stepping back. I look down at the three gold rings on my fingers and back to the skinny boys that won't even

look me in the eye. They are starving, and I'm wearing gold that my father gave me that could help them. I slide the rings off, putting them in the middle of the bread. One of the boys watches me the whole time, whereas the one with long, messy black hair doesn't look my way.

"Isola! Where are you?" I hear my mother shout, sounding worried.

"Goodbye," I say to them, but they don't reply as I turn around and run back to the carriage.

"YOU WERE the boy with the messy black hair," I say in shock. I hadn't thought I would ever see those boys again. I was so proud I had helped them, proud that I was like my mother and could do something beneficial for others. We made up stories in that carriage of how when I was queen, I could sneak out and feed the villages, even make some changes, so they weren't so hungry all the time.

"Dagan remembers you, just as I do, but he is too proud to thank you for saving our lives. Our mother had been killed by one of her clients, and the whorehouse had kicked us out that morning," he admits, the strain on his face suggesting it's hard for him to do so. I can see why Dagan would never bring it up, it must be a bad memory. I could only imagine how strong they both had to be to survive a life like that.

"I'm so sorry," I whisper, feeling a lot of respect for him.

"Don't feel sorry for me, princess. Your rings got us a room to rent in a house, where an old dragon guard found us and told us we had dragon guard blood. He trained us, and the rest is history," he says, looking down at the ground, much like he did when he was a child. Over the years, I had thought about those boys. I'd felt a connection to them that I've never really understood. I kind of get why my dragon likes Elias now, she must remember him and think he is someone important to her. *At least that's what I'm going to convince myself, and not that my dragon thinks he is the perfect mate for us.*

"My mother was killed two weeks after that," I say quietly and hold my Kindle closer to me as he looks back up. Our mothers were killed close to each other, our lives forever changed, and in so many different ways.

"What do you have on that?" he asks me, changing the subject. I hand him my Kindle after logging in, watching as he unlocks it. I can't even believe this place has Wi-Fi, but apparently it only works in here for some reason.

"All girly porn, the topless guys on the covers tell me that. This one even has three topless guys on it," he chuckles. "Interesting, what is reverse harem?" he asks me, giving me a look that would make most girls want to grab their Kindles and run.

"I'm not embarrassed about what I read, so stop looking like that. It's one girl with three or more men," I say, and he chuckles.

"Sounds like a lot of fun," he winks but then ruins it with his next words, "though I doubt someone like you could handle more than one guy."

"Just when I was starting to think you weren't a complete asshole," I say, snatching the Kindle back and setting it on the bookshelf behind me.

"I don't get why you read this stuff when real men are *much* better," he says.

"Maybe I read them because no men could ever compare to the men in these kinds of books," I taunt. I know my book boyfriends are all fictional fantasies, but still, it's true.

"Maybe you just have never found the right kind of man, *princess*," he says, stepping closer and making me rest my back against the bookshelves.

"I did," I whisper, and he tilts his head to the side.

"No, you didn't," he tells me.

"You don't know anything," I say, slamming my

hands into his chest. He laughs, grabbing both of my hands and pinning them above my head as I struggle against him.

"Let me go, Elias," I spit out, and he leans down, his head close to my ear.

"You may have loved Jacian, you may have *thought* he was everything to you, but he wasn't the man for you," he tells me, like he thinks he knows everything.

"How the fuck would you know anything?" I ask him, my dragon growl escaping my lips.

"Because you're still alive, still fighting for every breath, and your heart speeds up whenever I'm close to you. If he was the kind of love you would die for, the kind of love that burns away everything inside of you, you wouldn't be here now. You would be destroying the world for taking him from you. You wouldn't be able to think of anything other than revenge and death," he says.

"How could you possibly know that?" I reply quietly, hating that he could possibly be right.

"I had a woman I wanted to mate with, and I had to watch her die while I could do nothing to stop it. But I knew when she died, that I never really loved her, at least not like I should have. I still wanted to live after she was gone," he says.

"Then why did you want to mate with her? If you didn't love her?" I ask breathlessly, still pinned to the bookshelf, with his body pressed against me.

"I thought I did. I listened to my tutor when he told me our bloodlines would have made a powerful dragon guard, that we should be together because of our blood," he smiles, an almost sad smile. "Like you and Jacian were kept together, made to fall in love, because you were the last of the ice dragons. Not because you chose each other, or even loved each other."

"You may not have loved your mate, but I loved Jace," I snap.

"You did love him, sure, but you were never *in* love with him. There is a big difference, *princess,* and if anything, I hope you never fall in love with anyone. Because of who you are, you will lose them," he tells me, then lets me go. He walks off down the aisle as I try not to think about his words, though I know I will never be able to forget.

"You're quiet today," Korbin says as we run, and I don't immediately respond. Elias pissed me off way too much last night with everything he said, everything he made me think about. I know he was right, and I hate him for it. I did love Jace, but was I *in* love with him? Did I really even know the meaning? Every memory I have of Jace keeps flashing through my mind, and in not one of them can I really remember loving him. He was just there for me, and I kind of hate that Elias was right. We *were* pushed into being together. There wasn't another option. Everything was planned, from our first date at fifteen, to every date after that. We were such close friends, but I don't remember any moment that really made me think, I love this man. *I hate myself for these thoughts, it feels like such a betrayal.*

"I'm just tired, I didn't sleep well," I finally reply lightly, running faster to try and get the images out of my head that have been running on a loop all night. Thinking of my true feelings for Jace inevitably led to thoughts of his murder, and they have spiraled from there. Jace with the dagger in his heart. His dead eyes staring back at me. How similar he looked to my mother's dead body. They were killed in the same way, and I know I am next on the hit list. *Will I die just as they did?*

"Isola, watch out for the hill!" Korbin shouts at me. I'm so lost in my thoughts, I don't see the edge of the hill until I'm rolling down it. I scream as I hit trees, bouncing off them as I reach my hands out to try and grab onto anything, but it's pointless. I finally get to the bottom, rolling across the dirt and rocks, coughing as I pull myself up.

"Isola! Isola, I'm coming down!" I hear Korbin shout. Looking up, I see him jumping from tree to tree as he makes his way down the hill. *How the hell does he do that?* He jumps onto the tree closest to me, and slides down it, avoiding all the branches, and runs over to me.

"You're hurt, but it should heal," he says as he

grabs my chin to examine my cheek. I lift my hand, feeling the warm blood drip down my face as he shakes his head.

"What is going on in that head of yours that you weren't paying attention to where you were going?" he asks me, still holding my chin and making me look at his green eyes that are practically swirling with anger.

"Why do you care? This is just a job to you lot," I spit out, jerking my face away from him and walking a few steps away.

"I don't know why I give a damn about a spoilt fucking princess, but for some reason, I do. I don't see many other people lining up to be your friend," he says.

"Friend? You seriously want to be friends with someone you call 'a spoilt fucking princess'?" I ask, and he chuckles.

"That's right, doll, I do, and you look like you need a friend, but don't tell anyone that I'm yours," he warns, and I just laugh. The one person volunteering to be my friend, and he doesn't want me to tell anyone.

"Why should I trust you?" I ask him carefully.

"I never said to trust me–just that you can talk to me. I'm a good listener," he says walking over to me.

He takes my hand off my cheek, before quickly pressing it back.

"It's a deep cut, and my dragon senses that your ribs are broken. We'll need to stay here for about half an hour to heal," he tells me. I nod, already knowing that from the pain.

"Let's find a log or something to sit on then," I say as I place my other arm around my waist, and he nods. We walk silently through the woods for a little bit until we find a ring of logs. As we get closer, we notice the small, green plant in a pod in the center of the logs.

"What is that?" I ask, smelling something magical and pure, but not having a clue what it is.

"It can't be," Korbin whispers as he shakes his head, looking in absolute shock at the pod.

"Kor?" I prod. He rubs his beard, staring at the pod before looking at me and then back to the pod.

"You should touch it. If I'm right about what it is, it's here for you, not me," he says, looking at me in wonder.

"Is it dangerous?" I ask, and he shakes his head.

"I don't know exactly, but ancient magic is in the air, and it's not calling me. It's yours, whatever it is," he looks down at me. "Can't you feel the pull, doll?"

he asks as I look back at the pod. I do feel something that makes me want to walk over to it.

"Go, I won't let anything hurt you. I'm your dragon guard, and I don't feel danger here," he tells me. I know he can't lie to me about that, the curse won't let him put me in direct danger. It would be extremely difficult for him to get around it. I walk forward slowly, feeling the urge to touch the pod grow stronger with every step. *I wonder if I fell on purpose…I wonder what kind of magic is calling me.* This world was said to be full of magic years ago, both light and dark magic, but war destroyed so much of it over the years. It is said there is nothing pure left anymore, making dark magic more powerful than it's ever been. *But then, why does this pod smell so pure?* I was hidden on Earth to ensure dragons that use dark magic couldn't get to me. There is no magic on Earth, it doesn't work there for most people. I've heard of seers powerful enough to have magic there, but it's rare. I step into the circle of logs, kneeling down in front of the pod. I feel a force pushing from it as I lower my hand towards it.

"Be careful," Korbin warns, just as I touch it with my hand. I get thrown into the air, flying backwards, before smacking into a tree and sliding down. I open my eyes, and feel a burning sensation on my right hand. I lift it and see a green tree tattoo, right in the middle of my palm. It almost shines, a green glow emanating from it. I look over to see Korbin running towards me, but he stops when I stand, looking back at the pod. It's open, a small green fairy-type thing in the middle of it, fast asleep.

"What is that?" I ask as Korbin looks away from it and comes over to me.

"A baby tree spirit," he whispers and lifts my hand, swearing under his breath before dropping it.

"It has marked you as its own, and you have to look after it now. It's a blessing," he explains to me, staring in awe at the tree spirit.

"They are very powerful when they are older, blessed with magic. It's said the dragon they mark is destined for greatness. There hasn't been a dragon blessed by a tree spirit in thousands of years, doll," he says, looking down at me. He steps closer, rubbing a finger over my cheek. "It had to be you, didn't it?" he says so quietly that I'm sure he didn't mean to say it aloud.

"Kor," I whisper, wondering what he is thinking as he stares back at me. His eyes glaze over, fire burning across them for a second, before he shakes his head and steps away from me.

"The tree spirit must have healed you, your cheek

is completely mended. Pick her up, we can leave," he says, walking away to stare up the hill.

"Are we friends now, Kor?" I ask him.

"Seeing as we have cute little nicknames for each other, I would say so," he says, a hint of humor lacing his words that makes me chuckle a little.

"Can I call you Kor-Kor? Or Korby?" I ask. When he glares at me, I put my hands in the air. "Too far? Okay, I get it," I say, laughing as I walk over to the tree spirit. I lean down, scanning her long, glittering green hair, her pale green skin, and the tiny leaf she's wearing. She looks like a doll, albeit an odd one. Picking her up with both hands, I tuck her into my jacket and button it up, so she's tightly snuggled in.

"Let's go," Korbin says, pointing to the left of the hill.

"We need to walk this way for about half an hour, and then we can climb a small set of rocks to get to the castle," he tells me. We walk silently for a while, as I keep looking down at the tree spirit.

"There's a game called *The Sims*, and there's these plant *Sims* you can get in the game. She looks just like one, but with longer hair," I say, and Korbin gives me a strange look.

"What does the game do? We get a few games from Earth, but they are of no interest to me," he says.

"You make your own humans and houses. And you're able to control them," I explain.

"So strange, but I imagine that it is good practice for when you are queen and have a real world to control," he comments after clearly thinking about it.

"Not exactly. It takes hours to build a castle on that game, and there are no dragons," I say, and he gives me a confused look.

"I know, right? No dragons, no fun," I say, remembering how Jace used to think it was funny that I wanted dragons in the game.

"There's that look on your face, the same one you had when you fell," he says.

"I was thinking of Jace, you know the ice prince that is dead?" I repeat his words, and he flinches.

"I am sorry I said that to you. I have an excuse, but I doubt you want to hear it," he says.

"Tell me," I reply, kinda wanting to hear it.

"My girlfriend, intended mate, is here at the castle. I didn't tell her I was going to be here for a few weeks to protect you. I wanted to surprise her," he chuckles, a deep and dark chuckle that is a little frightening.

"What happened?" I ask, not understanding why I feel sick at the thought of him having a girlfriend. It's not like I could be interested in him like that. *He is a dragon guard; it's so forbidden it's not funny.* Besides, it's not like I can stop thinking of Jace, so it doesn't matter.

"I walked in on her screwing some dragon. She had the nerve to say it was my fault because I didn't tell her I was here," he growls.

"If you ask me, you are better off without her. She clearly didn't deserve you," I say, and he looks back at me for a second.

"After I found her, I came into the lunchroom, and I didn't think before I spoke. I can't apologize for Dagan, he is just a dick, but I didn't mean to upset you," he says.

"Apology accepted," I say, nearly tripping on a rock but able to catch myself. Korbin looks back, shaking his head.

"Come on, doll, before you break anything else," he teases. I grin, walking after him and deciding that maybe Korbin isn't that bad after all.

CHAPTER

FOURTEEN

ISOLA

F ire, fire, and more fire is everywhere I look. I can't see anything through the flames as they warm my skin. I look up and see the top of a building, strange lights hanging from the ceiling with wire hanging between them. This can't be Dragca. I feel myself turn around, and I see a figure walking through the fire. I run towards them, a sword in my hand that I hold up in the air.

"Don't," a female voice warns, and I stop, looking over to see a woman my age with black hair that touches the floor, a green dress, and black swirl tattoos on her face.

"Who are you?" I ask. I see the flames are frozen in place, and I look back at the woman.

"A friend, and what happened here, cannot happen," she smiles, and steps away. "This is your warning, my friend," she says, and then everything suddenly goes black.

I SIT up sharply in bed, holding a hand to my head and feeling like tiny daggers are being shot through my skull. *What in the world was that dream? This is the second one since I got here.* I jump when I hear a smash from my bathroom, followed by the sound of water being poured. I slide out of bed, walking slowly over to the bathroom, and open the door, not knowing what to think. The tree spirit has made a bath in the sink, with bubbles everywhere, and she is floating in it.

"Err, hello?" I ask, watching as she sits up in the water, swinging her hair around, and splashing water all over me.

"Bee," she says simply.

"Bee?" I ask.

"Bee," she says again, pointing at her chest this time.

"Is your name Bee?" I ask her. She nods, before swimming over to the plug and pulling it out as I just stare.

"So, Bee, you chose me or something?" I ask, and regret it instantly when it sounds like I'm quoting *Pokémon*.

"Bee," she says standing up as the water drains and putting her hands in the air. A ball of green glitter appears in her tiny hands, and she lets it go. It dries all her clothes as it lands on her, and she floats up into the air, flying past me back into my bedroom. I walk back into my room to see her land on my pillow, pulling my quilt over herself, and promptly going to sleep.

"That's rude, and cute. Hell, I don't know," I mutter, and I see her lips turn up in a little smile.

I groan when I realise it's Saturday, and I have history lessons or whatever with my uncle. I go into the bathroom and get ready, dressing in the leather uniform. I look back once more at a sleeping Bee before walking out. Thorne is leaning against the wall opposite my room, and he silently lifts a chocolate muffin and a coffee cup in the air.

"An apology muffin? I heard humans buy food to say sorry," he says, holding out his offerings. I accept them and laugh.

"Sometimes they do, but I've always preferred flowers or wine," I wink at him.

"Aren't you a little young in human years to drink?" he asks, but it's playful.

"I lived in Britain; the drinking age is eighteen, but they don't reinforce that much. I was drinking with Jace from fifteen," I say, thinking about how out of control we used to get because we knew we had so much responsibility in our future. It was just a good way to let off steam, to relax.

"When I mess up next time, I will remember the wine," he says, knocking my shoulder in a playful way. I eat my muffin, throwing the wrapper in a bin on the way to my uncle's office. It's clear everyone sleeps in on a Saturday, as we only see a few dragon guards as we walk. I drink the coffee slowly, wondering how Thorne knew I liked a lot of sugar in my coffee. *Thank god for dragon high metabolism, or I'd be the size of a house.*

"Good luck, and I will wait here, as usual," Thorne says, running his hand through his brown hair, before lowering it back to his side.

"Thanks," I smile at him before knocking on my uncle's office door and hearing him shout for me to come in. I open the door and walk in, seeing him sitting on his chair behind his desk. In the middle of the room is a map of Dragca. It's huge. I've seen maps of Dragca before, but this really shows the intricate details. It looks like a dragon eye. The main part is the land around the pupil of the eye, which is where we are. The pupil is mainly mountains, with two gaps in them. One is the castle my father lives in, and the other is the academy.

"Have you seen this map before?" my uncle asks.

"Yes, we had one sent with us when we were left on Earth. I have looked at it a few times, but never studied it," I say as he gets up and walks over to me. He picks a long walking stick up off the side of the wall and points the tip on my father's castle.

"The royal castle of Dragca, where you were brought up. It's on top of a mountain, making it impossible to penetrate from the ground. As you know, massive dragonglass spears are kept on the top of the castle, and the guards will shoot at any enemies that get close if the guards wish it. Not to mention the dragon guard who fly around defending the castle," he says, moving the tip of the stick across the map to the academy.

"This is us, and again, we are in a good position. We have dragons in the mountains, to keep us safe, but what is it that makes us safer than anywhere else in Dragca?" he asks me.

"I don't know, I think I remember something about a barrier," I reply, and he tuts.

G. BAILEY

"Every queen should know where to find the safest place in the world she rules," he warns me, and I nod, knowing he is right.

"Ten thousand years ago, there was a war between dragons and the dark magic users. When dragons use dark magic, it corrupts their souls, and there is no saving them. The dragons fought the war on the very ground we are standing on, but there was a huge price. We can't use light magic anymore. The abilities we were said to have, were lost that night," he tells me.

"What could we do? Why is it safe here?" I ask him.

"We could heal, we could see magic in the air, we could make portals, and most of all, we could connect to the magic of this world to do incredible things," he says and sighs. "Most magic is lost, as are the spirits we had as familiars and the magic they gave us. Dark magic still exists of course, but not dark familiars, so the dark magic users will never be that powerful," he informs me.

I start to tell him about Bee when my dragons whispers, *"Not to be trusted, must keep Bee safe,"* and I pause, closing my mouth before I say anything, deciding to trust my dragon. My uncle keeps talking anyway, not even noticing my pause.

"The land is safe because of the blood spilt here. It keeps those who want war and destruction away, literally stopping them from entering. Anyone that sides with the fire rebellion, would never be able to get in here," he says, and I nod. He slides the tip of the walking stick across to the land of the eye, and to the area just above.

"Any clue what all this is across here?" he asks.

"The poor villages," I say, remembering from my visit as a child. We flew across the purple ocean to them, and the villages are all the same from my memory. Mud huts, muddy ground, and full of the worst of our kind in some places, like the whore-houses and drug dens. There are also people who are just born into that life and don't deserve to be there, but have little choice. Not all dragons have rich parents, so they don't get an education or any way of escaping the life they have.

"A blight to our proud world, but every world has them," my uncles goes on.

"My mother used to say the most beautiful things in the world can be lost in the dirtiest and most dangerous places, which is why you should never give up hope," I say, remembering her telling me that before she tucked me into bed one night. She really was the sweetest person, so loving and kind.

"She was too kind for a queen, too full of hope, and it was her downfall," he says, and I turn sharply to look at him.

"Being kind is something a queen needs to rule fairly, and hope is something she should inspire in her people," I tell him.

"In a peaceful world, yes. In a world drenched in blood and war, no," he says and moves his walking stick to the left side of the map.

"This is where the fire rebellion live, in the old castles. They are able to see our every move with their army of seers. We cannot get too close to them, or they move around the castle so that it's empty when we do get there," he tells me.

"We have never fought with the seers before. How can we beat an army that can see our moves before we make them?" I ask, wondering about how it's even possible to win.

"That is something your father should answer, not me," he says and moves the stick to the other side of the map.

"What is here?" he asks me.

"Our farms. Our water farms and, well, every-thing we need to survive, comes from the East," I say.

"Correct. Without this, we would all starve. Or worse, our dragons would leave and go to Earth.

Could you imagine thousands of dragons appearing through the portals? It would be a war on Earth," he says, and he isn't wrong. That would be horrible, and the humans would never just accept dragons there. My uncle moves his stick to the bottom of the map, the black lands.

"What is here, Isola?" he asks.

"Nothing, just death and dead lands. No one can go there, ever, or they don't return," I say, knowing about those from the little I listened to Jace. He always wondered what made the lands dead, why they were lost.

"Your father sends traitors to the throne there, and you are right. You would never want to be there, Isola," he says and pulls his stick away. He rests it against the wall, and picks up a notebook and a pen.

"Here," he says, holding them out to me. I put my coffee cup down on the desk next to me and take them off him.

"I want you to write down the five main towns, the villages that surround them, and memorize them all," he tells me.

"There must be over three hundred villages, I couldn't possibly memorize them all," I admit.

"How do you expect to rule, if you don't even know the land," he shakes his head. "This is something you must learn, so get on with it," he says. I sit down on the floor, cross my legs, and start my list with the main cities. I know my uncle is right, and this is something I need to learn.

Mesmoia . . . Iaarita . . . Kenzta . . . .

"Bee?" I ask as I leave the door slightly open behind me and look at the empty place on the pillow, balancing my tray of food. I nearly drop the tray when I see the plant, well, now mini-tree, in my room. What was the small plant from my class, is now a blue tree with long leaves. There is a pod hanging from it and the pod has a door. *An actual door, do I knock?*

"Isola, I was just thinking–" Thorne says, coming into the room and stopping to stare at the plant, just as I am.

"What the hell is that?" he asks, quickly shutting the door behind him. I sigh and put the tray on my bed, knowing that I'm going to have to explain the tree spirit. I look at Thorne, who is watching me with surprise, and I wonder if I can trust him. I guess he has given me no reason not to.

"My tree spirit, Bee, must have made it grow and made herself a house by the looks of it," I say, and Thorne couldn't look more shocked if he tried. "Honestly, I don't know. I'm thinking about knocking on the plant door, but that sounds bloody weird," I say, and then laugh a little. I start shuffling my feet when it's silent between us for a long time, to the point of getting awkward.

"Thorne, are you okay?" I ask him, and he narrows his eyes at me. I step back as he walks over and grabs my hand, turning it over to see the tree mark.

"Why does it have to be you, *fucking you, of all people*," he growls, staring at the mark like his eyes could burn it away.

"Thorne?" I whisper, feeling like anything I may say could set him off right now. I don't know why he is so angry, but his hand is warming up and getting hot enough to burn anyone but me. When he looks up to meet my eyes, his are black. His dragon is in control.

"Thorne? Snap out of it, whatever this is," I tell him. He just growls at me, making me jump and try to move away, but his grip on my hand makes that impossible.

"You can't tell anyone about this, no one, Isola. I mean it," he says suddenly as he drops my hand. He seems to talk to his dragon before it fades away.

"*Mine,*" my dragon whispers in my mind, in such a silent whisper that I almost miss what she says.

"*You can't have every damn hot guy here, get over it already,*" I whisper back and glance up as Thorne's eyes turn back to normal.

"My dragon thinks this puts you in more danger," he explains, like it makes up for his behaviour. It's all confusing, when he shouldn't care, let alone his dragon.

"Korbin knows about my spirit, but no one else," I tell him, and he walks around me, looking at the pod hanging from the blue tree.

"I've never seen a light one. No one has, not in years," he says as he opens the door a little and stares inside. I move closer, leaning over his shoulder to see Bee sleeping on the base of the pod. She has a green leaf blanket covering her, and she is snoring lightly. *She is super cute.*

"She sleeps a lot," I shrug as Thorne shuts the door.

"My grandmother used to tell me she talked to the

tree spirits, and she used to leave sugary sweets out for them. She said they need sugar, it makes them happy and more active. Maybe she wasn't crazy like everyone thought?" Thorne says. I walk over to the pile of snacks, picking up a chocolate bar and opening it as I walk back. I break off two pieces and gently place them inside the pod, before shutting the door.

"Thanks," I say, feeling a little awkward after how he flipped out, and now is acting like nothing happened.

"No problem," he replies, rubbing the back of his head.

"Would you like to help me eat all this? And maybe hang out?" I ask. Thorne looks at the food and then back to me, clearly undecided.

"I guess I could eat," he shrugs. I climb onto my bed, moving the tray in the middle, as Thorne sits on the other side, putting his feet up. I watch as he pulls out a phone, a charged phone.

"Where did you get a charger? I can't find a plug anywhere except the library, and they only have Kindle chargers," I ask him.

"In here," he says, leaning up and opening a compartment in the headboard with a button that is shaped like a rose. Inside are three chargers, a row of different wires, and a spare iPhone that looks fully-charged.

"Holy shit, I think I love you," I say, sliding off my bed and going to my suitcase. I pull my phone out, and jump back to the bed to charge it.

"I think that's the first time a girl has said she loves me," Thorne comments, picking up a sandwich off the tray and opening it.

"I didn't mean–" I say, and he laughs.

"I'm joking, Issy, chill," he says, and I pick up some crisps and begin eating them.

"Tell me something random about yourself?" I ask Thorne, who finishes his sandwich and leans back on my bed.

"Why?" he asks me.

"I feel like we have only talked about our problems, and not what normal teenagers talk about," I comment. I know something happened with his parents, but we aren't close enough for me to have any right to ask him about it. I can see the shadows, the brokenness in his eyes, though he tries to hide it. I have a feeling Thorne has a lot of secrets hidden behind his hazel eyes.

"What do normal teenagers talk about? I don't think I've ever been one," he says.

"Okay, for starters, how old are you?" I ask.

"Twenty, and you're eighteen tomorrow," he says.

"Don't tell anyone that, I don't want to celebrate it. I never have liked my birthdays, to be honest with you," I say.

"Your secret is safe with me, but you might get a gift anyways," he grins.

"Don't," I throw a crisp at him, and he catches it, throwing it into his mouth while he grins.

"Favourite music?" I ask.

"The River Song, I loved to hear it as a child," he says, referring to the slow song that is played at mating ceremonies.

"I loved it, too, but I can barely remember it," I say. Automatically, I think back to the last mating ceremony held in the castle, the one where my father married my stepmother.

"It must have been hard, to watch your father remarry so quickly," he suggests, assuming when I must have last heard the song.

"I didn't understand back then, honestly. I was confused to see him with another woman, and I hated my father for it. I hated him more when I was taken to Earth and left alone for weeks until Jace was brought there," I say, and Thorne doesn't reply as we hear my phone buzz on. I lean up, pulling it down, but keeping it on charge as I unlock it.

"Jace," I whisper, seeing the photo of us laughing

at some party on the screensaver. Jace didn't like photos, but we both had been drinking, and he let me take this one. He looks so happy, charming, and everything I remember Jace being. I suck in a breath when Thorne leans over, wiping a finger across my cheek. I didn't even know I was crying.

"I was there, do you remember speaking to me? You asked me to make sure he had a dragon's burial?" he asks me.

"That was you?" I ask, remembering the young guard whose face I couldn't see, but he had given me that little time with Jace that I needed.

"Yes."

"Thank you," I say quietly.

"Don't thank me, Isola, just remember that you're not alone," he says, nudging my shoulder.

"Neither are you," I say, looking back at the photo of Jace, rubbing my finger over it. Despite how much I miss him, this picture seems to make it a tiny bit easier. It makes him seem more real, and not just a memory.

"Not even one smile?" Dagan asks after he and Korbin dragged me out of my room at four am. I rub my tired eyes, feeling particularly murderous this morning. It's my eighteenth birthday, and I'm out of bed at four am. That is not fair, not even one little bit.

"It's four in the fucking morning, no I'm not smiling," I state, crossing my arms, and carry on walking between them.

"Not a morning person then?" Korbin asks me, and I just groan.

"Breakfast?" I ask. *Food will make this morning livable.*

"Your dragon will hunt, there isn't any point of you having breakfast," Dagan says.

"My dragon doesn't hunt, or she never has before, at least," I tell him. He laughs, before he looks at my face and realises how serious I'm being.

"Shit, you're serious?" he asks.

"It's not like she is a vegetarian or something, but she is never interested in hunting. Jace used to hunt and bring it back for her while she watched," I say.

"Makes sense that your dragon is a little stuck–" Dagan goes to say, but a long growl from my dragon slips out, and he quickly rethinks it.

"You meant my dragon is lovely," I tell him. He smirks, not replying, just rolling that lip piercing between his lips instead.

"So, what are we doing in training?" I ask them.

"Flying, we will start off with flying and see if you can control your dragon," Korbin says as we get to a building outside the castle, where they've evidently been leading me. It's open-topped, and looks like an ancient arena with stone walls and stone seats.

"I have a little confession before we try this," I say when we get to the middle of the arena and stop.

"What?" Dagan asks me, and Korbin gives me a curious look.

"I haven't let my dragon out in . . . well, months,"

I admit, watching as they both give me matching looks of horror.

"You have no control over your dragon because you never let the poor creature out!" Dagan shouts at me, and I cross my arms, glaring back.

"I know, okay? I lived in the human world, where for years, all I worried about was who would win *I'm a Celebrity, Get Me Out of Here* and when I last checked Facebook," I say, completely avoiding the real issue with anything I could think of saying. I don't want to admit why I stopped letting my dragon out, that the loss of control scared the living daylights out of me the last time.

"What is *I'm a celebrity*?" Korbin asks, stroking his beard with his hand like he seems to always do when he is thinking.

"A show where they put famous humans in the jungle and film them. One wins, becoming queen or king of the jungle," I tell him. He looks over at Dagan, and then back to me.

"Do the others die? This sounds like it could be an interesting show," Dagan comments, and Korbin nods his agreement.

"No, they don't die. What is wrong with you two?" I protest.

"Shame, as that would have been funny to watch,"

Korbin says, and they both look at my disgusted face before they burst into laughter.

"Lighten up, princess, we have training to do," Dagan says, walking off, and still laughing. *Jackass*.

"I will shift first, and then Dagan, and then you," Korbin says, before walking a good distance away from me. I watch as he spreads his arms wide, a black mist covering his whole body. It gets bigger and bigger until a large black dragon slams its claws into the ground. Korbin's dragon has big green eyes, and a long neck with dark-red stripes down it. It spreads its large wings out, where I can see the red lines that spread down them.

"Amazing, so much red," I comment, and Korbin's dragon huffs a puff of smoke at me.

"I changed my mind, you shift first, princess, so I can watch in case something goes wrong," Dagan says as Korbin flaps his wings and flies up into the sky. I have to cover my eyes with my arm from the dust he blows at us.

"Fine," I say, taking my coat off and throwing it on the ground. I spread my arms out, whispering to my dragon.

"Will you fly with me and not take over?" I ask her, feeling her press against my mind. She doesn't answer me, instead just pushing for the change. I

scream as I fall to my knees, fighting her with everything I have.

"Answer me, or I will not let you," I demand. She roars, and it comes out of my mouth with a slight strangled feeling.

"Isola! What is going on?" I hear Dagan ask, and a pair of warm hands lift my face. I blink my eyes open, feeling tears run down my face as my body shakes, fighting my dragon. As I fight part of who I am, because I can't let this happen.

"I can't do this, I can't let her control me," I scream out, and she finally roars once more before backing down a little.

"What happened?" he asks me as the shaking calms down, and I feel my dragon sliding back under my control.

"I don't want to talk about it–" I say breathlessly.

"Isola, I need to know in order to help you," he demands, pulling my face, so I have to look at him. I focus on his dark hair; how perfect it is and the opposite of his brother's out of control hair. Dagan's serious look makes him even more addictive to stare at, but it's just the distraction I need to escape my head.

"Isola, tell me," he demands once more, and something makes me want to tell him. I never even told Jace, because I was so ashamed. I'm an ice dragon, it's part of me, and yet, I was powerless back then. And I've been scared ever since. *What kind of princess is scared of herself?*

"She killed a human, an old man in the forest, because she started to hunt him. I couldn't stop her, she wouldn't let me have any control back and wouldn't listen to me. The human was covered in blood from a cut on his head, he had fallen or some- thing, and once she got the scent . . ."

"She wouldn't stop, would she?" he asks, not saying the words.

"She didn't eat him, but the shock of seeing a dragon gave him a heart attack. She wouldn't let me shift back. I couldn't call an ambulance or help in any way. I just had to watch him as he died," I say, remembering how it was a student at school's grand- parent. I had to watch them cry, when I knew I could have helped. I could have saved his life if I had gotten help there.

"Have you talked to your dragon? Told her that's why you don't trust her anymore? That what she did was wrong," Dagan asks gently. He sits on the floor in front of me as he lets me go. I almost miss his touch when it's gone, and I have to shake myself from that thought.

"How would I know if I tell her it was wrong that she'd believe me? How do I trust that she listens to me? What if I let her take over, and she never lets me back?" I ask all these questions quickly, and then look away from Dagan's almost sympathetic face.

"I was training once when I was younger, and I read something in a study book on the relationship between us and our dragons," he pauses, "want to hear?" he asks, and I nod.

"Some people believe their dragon is like a demon that possesses their body, that they are two separate beings that live inside one person, but we know that isn't true," he comments.

"How?" I ask.

"They are us, and we are them. Dragon or person, animal or human, it doesn't matter. They are a part of us, and we have to protect them as much as they protect us, or we lose everything that makes us good," he says.

"You're quite wise for, like," I pause, "wait, how old are you?" I ask.

"Twenty-two, and you get wise in this world or you die stupid," he grins, jumping up and offering me a hand. I slide my hand into his, letting him help me up.

"I remember you," I say, feeling his hand tighten

around mine, and he pulls me close to him, a light growl coming from his chest.

"I don't owe you anything, don't expect a thank you," he warns me, already back to the asshole I've gotten used to.

"I don't want a thank you," I say, pulling away from him, but he doesn't let me go. Instead, he places his hand on my hip, pulling me closer to him.

"Yes, you do. Why else would you bring it up?" he asks me, still in a growly voice, though it's not as threatening.

"I said it because I wanted you to know, not because I expected anything from you, Dagan," I say, breathing as heavily as he is, both of us just staring at each other. Anger flits through me, as much as I think it's controlling him. Korbin's loud roar shakes us apart with a jolt. Dagan lets me go and walks away, running his hands through his hair. He opens his arms wide suddenly, and black smoke fills the space where he was as he shifts into a massive dragon. He is much bigger than Korbin's, with long red wings and black spikes on its back. It turns to look at me with its bright-red eyes, before turning around and flying up in the air. I hold a hand above my eyes as I look up to see Korbin and Dagan circling around in the sky.

"Let me fly with them, I miss my wings and being

free," my dragon whispers into my head with such sadness that I almost feel sorry for her.

"What you did, with the human, was wrong. You cannot ban me, as much as I should have never banned you," I admit. It was wrong not to sort this with her, not to let her inside my head. I know I should have done this much sooner.

"The human could have hurt you," she whispers, but I hear the guilt.

"No, he couldn't have, and you didn't trust me to make that decision. Promise me that will never happen again, that we work together, or this is all pointless," I tell her, feeling her sorrow in my mind, but she doesn't reply to me.

"We need to be strong to get revenge, to stay alive, and I'm not strong without you," I whisper.

"You are strong as you are me, but I promise to listen, to work with you. Now fly with mine," she insists, almost begging.

"Not mine, but alright we can fly," I reply.

"Mine," she states forcefully this time, and I shake my head.

"You can't collect hot guys like treasures, it doesn't work like that," I tell her.

"Why not?" she almost sounds like she is laughing in my head, and it makes me smile.

"Let's just shift," I say, needing to get her mind off the guys and onto something else. Her desire to have them, it's overwhelming me. I stand up, widening my arms and letting her take over. White smoke appears in front of me, blocking me from seeing anything as I relax, my body feeling like it's burning before she takes over. It's surreal watching my dragon run forward, stretching her long light-blue wings out, which are covered in ice, and taking off into the sky, as fast as a bullet.

"Free," she says as she goes further up into the sky and into the direction she can smell Dagan's and Korbin's dragons. They are flying around each other, flames coming off their wings as they flap them in the air, and they both turn towards me. My dragon lets out a long roar, icy breeze shooting out of her mouth, but it's not to harm them. They don't feel like danger to me. Dagan's dragon flies around me in a circle, before shooting off towards the mountains. I follow, feeling Korbin's dragon at my side, the wind pushing against my wings.

"Together," my dragon whispers, but I don't know if she means me and her together, or her and the dragons she keeps claiming as hers.

SEVENTEEN

ISOLA

"Y ou did well today, perfect even. Next week we will be training with swords, the week after flying, and so on," Dagan tells me as I pull my coat on. I look up at the dark skies, see the clouds and know it's going to rain soon. I raise my arms up and stretch, feeling all my muscles groaning.

"I forgot how tired shifting makes you," I reply.

"I like it," Korbin says, basically looking like he could go for a run or something. *Weirdo.*

"Want to have some fun and meet some of the students? It is your birthday, and you shouldn't be stuck in your room alone," Dagan asks me suddenly.

"How did you know?" I ask him, but Korbin answers.

"It's our job to know everything about you, to keep you safe," Korbin says, but he doesn't look at me as he says it.

"Alright, well, what kind of fun did you have in mind?" I ask them both this time.

"The bad kind," Dagan taunts. If I didn't know any better, I would think he was flirting with me. Maybe he just has that natural flirty nature some people have.

"There's a party out in the woods, they do it every month," Korbin explains.

"Will there be wine?" I ask.

"I know there will be beer," Korbin answers.

"Well, I'm sold then, let's go," I say, watching as they both smile at each other before we start walking towards the woods.

"Will Elias be there?" I finally ask, after we've walked in silence for a bit to get to the tree line.

"Yes, no doubt picking up a girl for the night," Dagan says, and I have to swallow the enraged rumble from my dragon.

"Kill the–"

"Oh my god, no, Dragon," I whisper to her.

"What is your dragon saying? Does she not like Elias?" Korbin asks me, clearly seeing the annoyance on my face and that my eyes have turned silver.

"Something like that," I reply, trying to avoid the question as much as I can. We come up to a clearing with a large bonfire in the middle. Some students are sitting on logs around it, and others are dancing to music from a speaker nearby. A few people stop what they are doing when they see me, just staring and looking none too friendly. They hate me because of my father, and the war, and maybe just because I'm not one of them. Oh, and I'm pretty sure me freezing the entire cafeteria didn't help with the whole people liking me situation. I may be a dragon, but I wasn't brought up here, and they know that. It makes me an outsider, in a place I don't need to be one.

"Maybe I should just go back to the castle, I need to get a new book from the library anyway," I say and start to turn back. Dagan puts an arm around my shoulder, drawing me back. It makes me go tense, whereas my dragon sends me waves of happiness. *Betraying little hussy.*

"Let me get you a drink and then introduce you to some people. You should try to get to know them," Dagan says, and I look over to see Korbin nod.

"He is right. You're pretty nice, sometimes, perhaps try to show them that?" he suggests, before walking over to some guys who pat his back.

"Alright, what's the worst that could happen?" I

shrug, letting Dagan lead me over to a cooler box. He opens it up, grabs two beers out, and hands one to me.

"They are a little warm as we have to hide them out here weeks in advance," Dagan says, and I chuckle. I grab his bottle off him and close my hands around both of our beers. I let my dragon out a little, making my hands go cold and cover the bottle in frost. I stop when they are cold, pulling my dragon power back and handing the bottle to Dagan.

"Neat trick," he comments, rolling his lip ring across his lips. I find myself focusing on it until he drinks some of his beer, and three girls walk over to us.

"Dagan! Have you seen Elias?" the blonde one in the middle asks. She has waist-length blonde hair with red streaks throughout it. The other two girls just spend the whole time eye-fucking Dagan, completely ignoring anyone else.

"Nope, how are you, Lisa?" he asks.

"I'm good, baby," she grins, stepping closer, and I move before I even noticed I'm doing it.

"I'm Isola, nice to meet you," I say after I've slid right in front of Dagan, and I hear him chuckle behind me. Lisa looks me up and down before putting on a fake smile.

"Lisa, nice to meet you, princess," she says and looks over my shoulder.

"Come and find me when your done with your *work*," she nods her head towards me with a snide look as she says work. I roll my eyes as she walks off.

"That didn't go well," Dagan says, stepping to my side as I drink my beer.

"You don't say," I reply sarcastically.

"Some might say you were jealous," he comments, watching me very closely for my reaction.

"And those same people would be wrong," I say, finishing my drink and reaching for another one. I pull the bottle cap off, chucking it in the box and walking off from Dagan, who is still chuckling. I stop when I get near the people dancing and down the rest of my drink, before sliding into the crowd. I close my eyes, dancing to the music and trying to forget everything. Trying to ignore how jealous it makes me to think of Dagan with that stupid girl.

"You're dripping snow on the ground, what's making you so mad," Dagan whispers in my ear, as his hands slide around my waist, pulling me against his toned body.

"How much have you had to drink?" I ask, still not opening my eyes but letting him control my hips, keeping our bodies moving in time to the slow music.

Every movement is sensual, and he knows what he is doing. *I hate that I like it.*

"Not enough," he whispers to me. We both dance silently for a long time, moving our bodies together like we know each other much better than we actually do.

"This isn't smart," I say, feeling how turned on he is as he's pressed against my back.

"No, it isn't," he agrees and breaks away from me. I turn in time to see him pushing through the dancers, his hands in tight fists at his sides. I mentally curse myself over and over as I maneuvre through the people and look around to see the castle in the distance. I can't see Korbin anywhere, or Elias, but I have a feeling he isn't here at all. My dragon can't smell him, or Korbin near for that matter. I walk away from the party, straight towards the castle as I try not to think about Dagan, Korbin, Elias, or hell, even Thorne. I should be thinking about Jace, my boyfriend who just died, and yet, here I am. My dragon is clearly already over him, but she is an animal, so it's expected in a way. She relies on instincts, not her heart, and I just can't process my own feelings right now. Whatever she is thinking can never be, because they are dragon guards. To let them love me, and allow myself to love them, it would break the curse, but they would lose their dragons.

"*Danger*," my dragon whispers, just before I hear a branch broken to my left. I stop in my tracks, sniffing the air. I don't catch a scent, but I trust my dragon.

"*Which way?*" I ask her.

"*Left,*" she replies, so I do the smart thing, and run to the right. I scream when a dagger flies past my arm, cutting my shoulder, and I nearly hit a tree with the distraction. Another dagger sails past my head, landing in the tree beside my head, and I duck around it. I look around as I keep running, seeing nothing but trees, and I realise that my best shot is to shift or shoot some ice at them.

"I got you," a voice says, just as I slam into a hard chest. I glance up to see Elias looking over my head. He pushes me behind him, and both his hands light up with fire. I jump when Elias darts forward, grabbing a dagger with a hand that's literally on fire. He spins, throwing the dagger back in the direction of my attacker. We hear a grunt, and then the sound of a body hitting the ground.

"Problem solved, are you okay?" Elias asks, the fire disappearing from his hands as he walks over to me. I lift my arm, turning it so I can see the cut isn't healing.

"It must have been dragonglass, or I would have healed by now," I comment, and my eyes widen as Elias pulls off his shirt. The tattoos I have seen on his arms also cover his entire chest. There's a large red dragon across his ribs, and a row of symbols I don't recognize over his heart that continue all the way down his v line into his jeans. *I wonder where they stop.*

"Don't get too excited, we need to stop the bleeding," he laughs at my wide eyes, which I narrow as he steps closer.

"Eh, I've seen better," I shrug, trying to ignore the six pack on display, and the way his chest is so toned. Bloody hell, all I can think of is licking it. *There is something seriously wrong with me.*

"Really? Somehow, I doubt it, my naughty princess," he chuckles, brushing his naked chest against my body as he lifts my arm.

"Try not to scream, this might hurt," he says, as he wraps the shirt around my arm, and then pulls hard. I rest my head on his shoulder as I try not to scream, but a whimper escapes despite my best efforts.

"That will stop the bleeding, but I bet your tree

spirit could heal it up for you," he says, and I lift my head off my shoulder to meet his dark eyes.

"How did you know?" I ask.

"I broke into your room tonight because I smelt a dragon in there that shouldn't have been. It seems your little tree spirit had put a barrier up anyway, so I couldn't get in. I followed the scent of the dragon out here, and I'm glad I did," he comments.

"You broke into my room?" I ask.

"Out of everything I just said, that's the bit you're focused on? Technically, I just walked in, as the door was open from the dragon that broke in first," he replies.

"I suppose it's not that bad then," I say dryly. He laughs and steps closer to me, boxing me in against the tree at my back.

"There's just something about you . . . what is it that draws me in?" he asks, making my breath catch. I can't escape or look anywhere other than into his eyes.

"Is it you or your dragon that is interested?" I ask, wondering how much of him is in control, because his eyes are naturally dark, and I can't tell.

"My dragon and I are divided on you, princess," he says, and goes to say something else, when we hear Korbin shout.

"What is going on here?" Elias moves away from me, and I look over to see Korbin standing watching us, blatant anger all over his face.

"Kor . . . I need you to take the princess to her room. She is hurt, and I need to deal with the body of the attacker," Elias says.

"Hurt? What the fuck happened, Eli?" Korbin demands, somehow looking even angrier than before as he walks over to us. He steps right in front of me, lifting my arm.

"Ow, that hurts," I say, pulling my arm away.

"We can't leave her alone, nowhere is safe, apparently," Korbin tells Elias, who looks at me for a long time before answering.

"You need to stay with her tonight, and I will find Dagan and explain. We should sleep in her room for protection now," Korbin comments.

"That's not–" I go to protest, but they both ignore me.

"I don't want a damn roommate!" I shout at them, and they finally pay attention to me.

"Well, you have three now, get over it," Elias says.

"Four, you're forgetting Thorne," I say, not knowing why I feel I have to remind them.

"He can't be trusted," Elias says, but Korbin shakes his head.

"With her, he can, trust *me* on that," Korbin says. They stare at each other for a while before Elias gives in.

"Take her back. I'm taking the body to her uncle," he says and walks off into the forest. I stare after him, until I can't see any trace of him anymore. *What is Elias Fire doing to me?*

EIGHTEEN

W *hat the fucking hell is wrong with me?* I can't get the image of Elias pressed so close to Isola out of my head. My dragon was ready to fight him, one of my oldest friends, over a girl that isn't mine. *A girl that can never be mine because of the curse.*

"Elias thinks Bee will heal me," Isola says quietly, as we climb up the steps of the castle, heading towards her room.

"Bee?" I ask her, having no idea what she is going on about.

"Bee is the tree spirit's name, or what she told me," Isola shrugs.

"Interesting, so she can speak?" I ask.

"Not exactly, she's only said Bee," she chuckles,

her laugh light and sweet. It's annoyingly attractive, but then everything about her is. From her shiny, soft-looking blonde hair to her curvy body that I find my eyes admiring far too often. We get to her door before I have to answer her. I open it, seeing the massive blue tree first.

"Did Bee do that?" I ask, closing the door behind us and walking over. The tree has a green pod hanging from it, and it has an actual little door on it.

"Yep, on her first night. I'm meant to take the plant back to the teacher with knowledge on what it does," Isola says as she sits on her bed and starts undoing Elias shirt, "but I can't take that tree back. I can't even move it, and I still have no idea what it does."

"I can help you find out. You need to test the leaves or any fruit it makes," I say, stepping closer to the tree and stroking a blue leaf. The door to the pod bursts open, and Bee pops her green head out, looking up at me.

"Isola needs you," I tell Bee, who immediately flies out the door and straight over to Isola. She lands in Isola's lap, and I watch as they stare at each other.

"You don't have to help me; I'm sure I can sort it out myself," she tells Bee, who flies around Isola, looking for something before flying back over to the tree. She goes inside her pod, and comes out with a tiny white bag.

"Where did you get a bag?" Isola asks.

"Bee make," Bee answers in a tiny voice.

"Remember that elder tree spirits make dragon clothes, woven with magic. It makes sense that Bee could make small items," I comment.

"Bee," Bee says with a happy nod, and flies over to Isola. I watch as she gets a handful of what looks like glitter, and sprinkles it onto Isola's arm above the cut.

"Damn, that hurts," Isola whimpers, as she closes her eyes. I walk over, kneeling in front of her as Bee keeps sprinkling the magic powder on the cut. I take Isola's hands in mine, letting her squeeze them as tightly as she needs.

"Sleep," Bee comments, just as Isola falls forward onto my lap, and I catch her, lifting her in my arms. She tucks her head into my shoulder, her lips brushing my neck as her breathing gets heavier.

"Bee done," Bee comments, making me look away from Isola and watch as she carries the bag back to her pod, and slams the door closed behind her. *That's one interesting tree spirit.*

I slip onto the bed, rolling Isola down next to me as gently as I can, remembering to make sure she doesn't sleep on her hurt arm. She immediately cuddles into the pillow as I reach down to take her shoes off. I pull the blanket up, tucking her in, and she whines softly in her sleep. I don't know what I'm thinking as I stroke a finger down her cheek, and tuck a little piece of her hair behind her ear.

"Sleep well, doll," I comment quietly, and look at her arm before moving away, seeing it's nearly completely healed.

"Thanks, Bee," I whisper to the pod as I walk past and go over to the window seat. I look over at Isola, seeing how peaceful she looks as she sleeps. You wouldn't know she was just attacked a few hours earlier. I like that about her, that she doesn't destroy herself because of everything that's happened to her. It must have been soul-crushing to lose Jacian, the boyfriend she grew up with and likely loved. *What would have happened if he lived?* I doubt the fire rebellion would have as much support if there were two heirs to the throne. I get as comfy as I can before closing my eyes and trying to drift off to sleep, when someone knocks on the door. I groan, getting up and walking over, pulling it open to see Dagan on the other side. He pushes into the room, heading straight over to Isola and looking down at her.

"Is she alright?" he asks me, his voice gruff and deep, almost a growl.

"She's fine," I say, shutting the door. I wait for him to notice the tree spirit, but he doesn't look away from Isola for a long time.

"It was my fault; I left her out in the woods, and I damn well shouldn't have. I knew you had gone back to the castle, and I still left her alone," he says.

"They would have gotten to her either way," I comment, knowing whoever it was would have planned some way to get her alone.

"I saw the body, it was a student. Her uncle has sent the guards after his family and kicked his brother out of the school, just in case," he says. I hate that the punishments for attacking the throne are so high. There is a good chance his family didn't know anything about the attack on Isola, but her father won't care. He kills anyone that is an enemy, no matter what.

"Damn," I comment, running my hand over my beard as I look away.

"And when the fuck did she get a tree spirit?" Dagan asks, pointing at the pod and knowing straight away what it is.

"Bee, the tree spirit, marked her when we were on a run. I think Isola might even be able to use light magic, but I haven't told her yet. It's probably not a good idea when she needs to be in perfect harmony with her dragon before even attempting magic," I say, looking back at Isola. She could be the most powerful dragon in years if she is able to use light magic. She could be the most powerful queen Dragca has ever seen.

"Light magic and tree spirits, it all sounds like fairy tales. There hasn't been a tree spirit familiar in thousands of years, or a dragon that can use light magic," Dagan replies.

"They say that when dark magic rises, light magic will rise to fight it," I say as Dagan steps away from the bed.

"I don't know a thing about magic, but I don't like this. It doesn't feel right," he tells me.

"Nothing has felt normal since Isola got here. Something feels wrong, and I know that," I reply, "but we have a job to do, and we can't focus on anything else until it's done," I remind Dagan.

"I will see you in the morning after your run," he calls as he walks out of the room. I go back to my window seat, laying my head back, and getting some much-needed sleep.

NINETEEN

ISOLA

T wo hands grab my face tightly, almost hurting me, as I hear a voice shouting, but I can't understand it.

"Who?" I ask, looking up to see a blurry face staring down at me, mouthing words I can't really understand.

"I know you think you hate me, but not like this, not before I can tell you how much of a fucking idiot I am," the man says, but I can't make out who it is.

"I hate you," I spit out, but for some reason, it feels like I'm lying.

"No, you don't, and you do hate that," he replies, before picking me up, and I look away from him. He walks us through a room I can't see, it's all blurry, but

I look over to see the same girl from my last dream is standing in the middle of the room.

"Remember this moment, he is not all evil," she says vaguely. I want to shout at her, demand to know who she is and why she keeps coming into my dreams.

"Who?" I ask, only able to get one word out. I don't even know if I mean her, or the man holding me.

"Yours, always yours," the man replies as my head rolls to the side, and I feel like I'm falling.

I open my eyes to my bedroom. Unhooking my arms from my pillow, I sit up feeling amazing. I honestly feel like I've drank ten energy drinks or something, and that isn't normal for me in the morning. I nearly jump when I see Korbin sleeping on my window seat, looking relaxed and peaceful. I look down at my leather outfit, and see that someone took my boots off last night and tucked me in. I look at my arm, seeing a little white scar and some dried blood, but other than that, it's all healed. *That's incredible.* I slide out of my bed, stretching as I walk over to Korbin, hovering my hand over his shoulder, ultimately deciding not to touch him because that might be a little weird.

"Did you sleep on my window seat all night?" I ask Korbin as he opens his eyes and looks over at me from the weird angle he is resting at against the window. His brown hair is messier than I've ever seen him, actually making him look relaxed, and less serious than I'm used to. He looks cute in the morning, but I'd best not tell him that.

"Pretty much," he yawns, standing up and stretching out.

"Can we skip the run today?" I ask hopefully, and he laughs.

"Nope. I'm going to my room to shower, and I'll bring back breakfast," he says, walking around me to the door.

"Thank you for looking after me; I know you didn't have to," I say, and he laughs.

"I'm your dragon guard, of course I have to," he reminds me. I feel stupid for thinking he stayed because we are friends, not because he felt he had to stay. I wonder if that's how they all feel–Dagan, Elias, and Thorne. I'm just a job to them, work, like Lisa said last night. I turn away and walk to the bathroom, shutting the door behind me. I switch the shower on, stripping all my clothes off and getting in. There's something about a hot shower that lets you calm down, and makes everything seem a little bit better for some reason. I try to remember the girl in my dreams, who has said such weird things, and wonder how she can even get into my dreams in the first place. But none of the ideas I come up with make any sense. I wash my hair before getting out of the shower, plaiting it, and then getting into my active-wear clothes. It's really weird how they are clean and folded every morning. I pull my trainers on before getting a chocolate bar out of my chest of drawers, and breaking the pieces up, placing them gently in the pod where Bee is sleeping. She doesn't even notice me open her door.

"Thanks for last night, even though it hurt, there's no lasting mark or anything," I whisper, and one of her eyes opens slightly.

"Bee help," she yawns, and then pulls her green leaf sheet closer around herself and rolls over. Clearly that's the end of that conversation. I walk out of my room, stopping when I see Thorne and Korbin talking quietly. They instantly stop their conversation when they notice I've come out, and look me over.

"Hey, guys," I smile, feeling more awkward by the second as they continue to stare. Thorne snaps out of it first, walking over and lifting my arm, turning it to see no mark.

"I didn't know until this morning, and Korbin said you are okay. I'm sorry I wasn't there. I failed you, failed as your guard," he says angrily.

"You couldn't have known," I reply.

"Still, I think Elias' plan to have someone with you at all times is for the best," he says.

"I have been called to see your uncle, to tell him everything I can about last night, and what our plans are from here. Thorne has offered to take you to class, and we can skip running for today," Korbin says, passing me a paper bag and a bottle of orange juice.

"She prefers coffee," Thorne comments.

"Duly noted," Korbin laughs, patting his shoulder before walking off.

"We have an hour before class, anything you want to do?" Thorne asks me as I lean against my door, drinking the orange juice. Opening the bag, I peek inside and see a cinnamon roll.

"What do you usually do?" I ask him.

"Training," he shrugs.

"What kind of training?" I prod as I start eating the cinnamon roll, and he sighs.

"Why don't I show you instead of trying to explain? It will just sound dorky if I don't," he says and walks off. I jog to catch up with him, chucking my empty bag and bottle into a bin as we go past.

"Have you been studying?" he asks me.

"Nope, being attacked and all this training has been a little bit of a distraction. I haven't even gotten my books out my locker from my first day," I admit, and he shakes his head.

"You need to study, that's all I'm saying," he comments, and I whack his arm with the back of my hand.

"Don't be so . . . so, erm . . . annoying and teacher-like," I say, making him laugh.

"You don't find me annoying, though," he grins as he opens the front door to the castle. We walk across to the arena in silence, with me not sure how to reply to him without lying. He is right. I don't find him annoying at all, and that's a real issue. I shouldn't find him anything, he's just Thorne. Thorne with his brown hair, his hazel eyes, and impressive body. Thorne who is kind and yet dark in a seductive way that makes you want to figure him out.

"Do you have a favourite weapon?" I ask him.

"I'm about to show you mine."

"If you show me yours, that doesn't mean I will show you mine," I say, joking with him a little, and he laughs.

"When you want to show me yours, Issy, I promise you can see mine," he winks at me before opening the doors to the arena as I stand in utter shock from his flirting. I don't know how serious he is, but, holy crap, my dragon seems to like the idea, judging by the way she is purring in my mind. I walk in, following Thorne straight across the arena and to the other side, where there is a row of targets set up.

"Bow and arrows? I should have guessed, considering you don't carry around swords like Korbin and Dagan, or daggers like Elias," I comment.

"And you don't carry any weapons at all, Issy, not the best idea," he says.

"On Earth, it's not normal to train with swords or daggers. I did self-defense classes with a Bo staff, and some archery classes, but I was never very good at either," I confess to him.

"You should be, with your dragon sight," he gives me a confused look.

"I've never used it," I admit. I know that you can tap into your dragon's eyesight and focus on things, but Jace and I never had anyone to teach us that. We had to learn everything from flying to hiding by ourselves. I know it was because we were safer away from any dragons, but that doesn't mean we didn't struggle to fit into a world we weren't meant to be in. I wonder how Jules is, if she has moved out or just carried on her life.

"Really?" he asks, and I nod, "Let me help you," he says, picking up a silver bow and five arrows in a quiver that he slides on his back. Thorne brings them over to me, and we walk over to an 'x' marked on the floor a good distance away from the target opposite us.

"Stand sideways, and hold this," he instructs me as he offers me the bow. I stand how I remember being told in archery classes, and suck in a breath when Thorne's warm hand adjusts my waist, as he steps behind me.

"This way a little," he says and then offers me an arrow. I nock the arrow and lift the bow, lining the arrow up with my lips and keeping it close to my cheek as I was taught when I was younger.

"Now, don't call your dragon, just focus on her eyes in your mind, only picturing her glowing blue eyes. Focus only on them," Thorne whispers in my ear, his body still so close to mine. I struggle to focus on anything other than the way Thorne is holding me, though I know I need to forget he is here for a moment. I close my eyes and take a deep breath, focusing on my dragon's eyes like Thorne suggested. I imagine the glowing blue I've seen in my reflection when I've looked into a body of water. I open my eyes, suddenly feeling a change spreading across them. Everything is super-focused when I look around, and I move my bow to the left a little. I can see the direction it will fly, like it's mapped out in my mind, and I let it go. It flies straight into the middle of the target as I release my dragon's power.

"That was amazing, thank you!" I exclaim, dropping the bow and turning to throw my arms around Thorne's neck. He holds me close, his hands on my waist as I lean back.

"Seriously, thank you. I didn't know it was like that," I tell him, and he just stares down at me.

"No problem," he says gruffly, and draws back from me, reaching inside his cloak. He pulls out a small blue box, and offers it to me.

"I can't wrap anything, but I saw this and thought of you," he says as I accept the box. I open it up to see a small ring, silver dragonglass by the feel of it. The ring has a frozen blue swirl, with blue leaf-shaped crystals on it. I slide it onto my finger, feeling my dragon's love for it as much as my own.

"Thank you! As you know, all dragons love shiny things," I say.

"You shouldn't have a birthday without a gift. That's all it is," he says, and I look up, both of us locking eyes with each other momentarily. I can't tell what's going on from his eyes as he walks away.

"Thorne, wait!" I shout after him, but he doesn't stop. *What just happened?*

TWENTY

"**Y**ou are extremely late, Miss Dragice," my uncle scolds me as I walk into class. I mentally groan when I realise he is my teacher, and this had to be the class I was late for. Of all the damn classes.

"I got lost," I say, telling him the truth. After Thorne left me in the arena, apparently not giving a crap about my security, I had to figure out which class I had and how to get there. Not an easy feat. Thankfully, I found Korbin in the corridors, and he took over guard duty and taking me to class. *I need to find a damn map of this place.*

"Sit down now," he demands, and I glance around the room at the ten or so students in the class before finding a seat in the middle of two girls and quickly sit down.

"We shall start from the beginning to see if any of you were listening, I want each of you to tell me something about each race," he says, and there are several groans. I don't even need to look around to know everyone in this class now hates me even more than they did before.

"Welcome, Miss Dragice, to the Races class. We study each of the races that lives in Dragca, and we even spend some time studying humans, which I'm sure you will excel in," he says with a small smile at me. "Now, who can tell me about the seers' race? That was what we were discussing before Miss Dragice came in," he asks, and the girl next to me puts her hand up. She has long red hair, and her hazel eyes narrow on me before she answers.

"The seers have been around as long as the dragon race has, as long as humans have been around on Earth. Seers cannot shift, they have human life spans that are not extended like ours, and their magic comes from Dragca itself," she says.

"All correct, Miss Lamar. Seers are powerless on Earth, the very magic they need is lost to them if they travel over. Now, anyone else?" he asks, and a guy near the front puts his hand up.

"Seers have different bloodlines that determine

their powers. Some can only see the future and others the past, and then there are seers that can warn their family of events that will happen as well as seeing the future. They only usually see the future of their close family members," he says.

"How do they warn their families?" I interrupt, and the class all looks at me, but it's my uncle that answers.

"Dreams. Seers can connect with their close blood relatives through dreams," he tells me, and I sit back in shock. I don't hear anything else they say as I think back on the dreams I've had since I got here. They aren't fake. The girl close to my age in my vision must be a seer, and she must be a relative of mine. What's worse are the dreams she showed me, this means they have to be real, and not a single one of them looked like anything good.

"Now, come and get a textbook from the front, and I want you to find something new to tell me about seers from it by the end of class," my uncle says, and I get up robotically to get a textbook as my mind goes over and over who the girl is and how she is related to me at all. *Dragons and seers cannot mix, it's never been heard of . . . but how else can she exist?*

"HEY, WATCH IT," Elias calls out, as I bump into him on the way to the library after class. He grabs my shoulders to stop me from walking away from him.

"Where is Thorne? He is meant to be watching you today," Elias asks.

"I don't know, we–" I start to explain, but I honestly don't know how, "it doesn't matter," I reply, and he lets me go. I walk away, only to have him fall into step next to me.

"Don't you have dragon guard things to be doing?" I ask him, and he shakes his head.

"I trained all morning," he grins, "so, where are we going?"

"The library, I want to find some books on seers and the bloodlines, then to my locker to get my text books, so I can study," I tell him.

"What do you want to know about seers?" he asks, more seriously this time.

"It's nothing," I shake my head, trying to walk faster, but he catches me around the waist. He pushes me against the wall and presses his body into mine, holding my hands above my head.

"Let me go," I seethe, shocked that he could maneuvre me into this position so damn quickly.

"No, because you lied to me, and I don't like it. Now tell me what you're doing, and I might help you, my naughty princess," he says, making me growl at him.

"I'm not your naughty princess, stop calling me that! It makes it sound like I do naughty things to you," I reply. Elias chuckles darkly, pressing his body harder into mine, and I hate that he smells so good, and feels even better against me.

"We could, it wouldn't have to mean anything. As long as I don't fall in love with you, which would never happen, the curse wouldn't be triggered," he suggests, leaning his head down, so our lips are just inches apart. I lift my knee and slam it into his balls. He groans and falls to his knees, letting me go as he drops.

"Dragon or not, that had to hurt as much as your ego will when I tell you I'd rather fuck myself," I fume. I will never be someone's fuck buddy, especially when they don't respect me. If I decided to sleep with anyone, it would be because I want to and because it meant something. I may be old-fashioned like that, but I don't care. Plus, I have a feeling Elias would end up crushing my heart, whether he meant to or not, when he walked away from me, which he already said he would.

"Isola, wait," Elias shouts after me as I hurry away. I'm kind of glad no one is around.

"Fucking wait!" Elias yells after me again. I hear him right behind me seconds before he jumps in front of me and places his hand in the air to stop me.

"I'm a douchebag, and I'm sorry. I fancy you, alright? My dragon does, too, and he is flooding me with desire for you," he says. "I'm not thinking straight right now."

"I get it, my dragon isn't any better," I say, "but fucking isn't a good idea. I've never slept with someone that I wasn't in love with, and I won't start now," I say firmly. I know I'm worth far more than that.

"No one-night stands? Just for the pleasure?" he asks, flirting again.

"I'm eighteen and lived with my boyfriend until he died, so no," I say, and he steps closer.

"Friends, then? Even if we fancy the pants off each other?" he says with a wink.

"Friends, just friends," I say, shaking the hand he offers me.

"Now, about the seer bloodline, explain what you need to your *friend,* because he might have had a seer friend as a kid and know some shit about them," he grins, making me chuckle.

"Of course you did, but I don't think we should talk here," I gesture to the empty corridor.

"My room then," Elias says, not waiting for my answer as he turns around. I know I need to follow him for the answers I need, despite my hesitance. I guess I can't go through life never trusting anyone, though Elias Fire might not be the best dragon to trust. But, I guess a part of me does anyway, because I walk after him.

CHAPTER

TWENTY-ONE

ISOLA

"**Y**our room is much brighter and cleaner than I expected," I mutter, eyeing the light-blue sheets on the big bed, matching curtains, and the white rug. There's a wardrobe, a box by the window seat with a pile of notebooks on top of them. But everything is put away and in order, there are no clothes on the floor or rubbish anywhere.

"What did you expect?" he asks as he shuts the door.

"Black everything, posters of half-naked women, and dirty clothes on the floor," I reply, and he laughs. He takes his swords off his back and places them near the door. One of the swords is black and the other a dark-red. They are kind of beautiful to look at. I watch as he pulls his jacket off, and then his boots, putting them neatly by the door.

"Sorry to disappoint, princess, but I like my shit sorted," he says with a grin. I walk around his room, lifting one of the notebooks up and looking over at him.

"May I?" I ask him.

"Sure," he nods, and I open the book up. Inside are pages and pages of tattoo designs, some in 3-D and others not, but they all are so amazing. There are roses, dragons, and one of several vines swirled around inside a circular drawing.

"Did you design these?" I ask.

"Yep. I designed my own tattoos, as well as Dagan's and Korbin's. Maybe you will let me design yours, and I could take you to my friend for a tattoo," he suggests with a wicked smile.

"The princess covered in tattoos? That would be interesting, and I think my father would kill you."

"So? Do you always play by the rules?" he teases as I put the notebook down.

"Maybe one day," I chuckle.

"I'll design you something," he says in a cocky tone, and I shake my head at him, knowing he won't give up.

"Tell me everything," he says, jumping onto the

bed and patting the space next to him. I slide my boots off before sitting next to him and he grins over at me.

"You could lie down," he suggests with a wink.

"I'll sit," I say, ignoring his flirty tone. *Didn't we just say friends only?*

"I've been having dreams since I got to Dragca, of random things I don't understand, but there's always this girl in them. I've realised they are visions of my future, and she says they are warnings for me," I say, watching as his eyes widen. He sits there, seemingly speechless for a little bit.

"Shit," he draws out the word. Elias turns on his side, opening the drawer in his bedside cabinet and pulling out a box of cigarettes.

"Those aren't good for you, they kill humans, you know," I comment.

"Lucky I'm not human then, isn't?" he says and gets a cigarette out, lighting it up and resting back against his bed.

"She must be related to you, a close relative in order to be able to give you warnings," he muses, "but that is unlikely, seers and dragons can't have children," he says.

"How do we know that, though? It's only what we have been told, and I can't see any other way this seer is contacting me," I say, frustrated. I watch him as he thinks, inhaling deeply from his cigarette and blowing it out slowly.

"Nothing is impossible, not ever," he says, eyeing me closely.

"Some things are," I answer.

"I don't believe that," he shakes his head.

"Are we still talking about me having a seer relative?" I ask.

"What else would we be talking about princess?" he grins at me before looking away.

"*Anyway*, I don't think I should tell anyone until I can talk to her some more," I say.

"You shouldn't tell anyone. The fire rebellion already claims to have another heir and this would give them more fire to burn you with," he says.

"How do you know that?" I ask.

"Everyone knows it, everyone is talking about the heir that no one has seen."

"This seer could be an heir and have a claim to the throne . . ." I taper off and lean back on the headboard of the bed.

"What did she look like?" he asks me, putting his cigarette out in an ashtray on the bedside cabinet.

"Long black hair, my age, blue eyes," I tell him, shrugging. "She doesn't look like an ice dragon. She isn't blonde, and from what I remember, her eyes aren't that pale," I say.

"Strange. When I lived in the castle here, there was a seer that was the son of one of the teachers. He was a good guy, and we hung out a lot," he tells me.

"That's how you know about seers?" I ask.

"Yep. He told me a lot of shit, and the most important bit here is," he leans closer to me, dropping his voice, "seers can only contact very close blood relatives with warning: sisters, brothers, mothers and fathers. No one else, because the magic doesn't allow it," he says.

"Impossible, my mother didn't have any other children, and my father would have told me," I shake my head and lean away from him.

"Would he?" Elias challenges me.

"Don't. My father wouldn't lie to me about another heir," I say, shaking my head.

"You don't know him, princess. You haven't seen him in years and have no idea what he is like now," he says.

"I remember–" I start to say, but he stops me.

"Exactly. You remember the father that was mated to your mother and happy. We all know the king who had to give his daughter up after losing his mate, and then savagely hunted fire dragons in order to find out who killed her," he contends. I move to get off the bed, not wanting to hear this, when he grabs me around the waist, slamming me onto the bed and holding me down.

"Get off, I don't want to hear this, Elias," I protest, struggling to get up.

"You need to listen, princess," he insists, as he leans down, and I turn my head away from him.

"I do not," I spit out.

"Do you even know what started the war? How many innocent fire dragons your father killed in the name of your mother? How many dragon guards have died protecting him from the angry families of the fire dragons he's killed?" he asks me.

"Enough!" I shout, feeling my hands freezing the bedsheets under us.

"You don't know a thing, princess, and you do *not* know your father," he tells me, and I look back up at him with tears in my eyes.

"Kings often must make difficult choices, and yes, he might have been wrong. I don't believe he is evil. He is my father," I implore him to understand.

"And all you believe you have left," Elias says softly, searching my eyes for something. I hate that it seems like he can see more in my eyes than I want him to.

"He *is* all that I have left. I don't have anyone else, Eli," I say, and he closes his eyes. When he opens them again, fire burns the colour away, leaving them black.

"I like that, when you call me Eli," he whispers.

"Eli?" I ask when he suddenly jumps off me, climbing off the bed. I sit up and watch his rigid back in the tense silence in the room.

"You should leave before I listen to my dragon and say screw the friends rule we made, princess," he warns me. He never looks at me once as I get off the bed and grab my things. I pause at the door, glancing back at Eli with his head lowered and arms crossed.

"Bye, Eli," I whisper, and his black eyes dart up to gaze at me. I turn and open the door, walking out before I say anything else stupid.

"Another warning?" I ask the shadowy figure in the room full of ice I find myself in. The floor, walls, and the ceiling are all frozen. I look down at my white dress, it's covered in glitter and crystals.

"Yes," the girl says, as her body comes into focus, and I can see her blue eyes, dark hair and the long, dark-blue dress she has on.

"Of what? Ice?" I ask, and she laughs sadly, shaking her head.

"Of what happens when fire falls for ice," she waves around the room I don't recognize, "ice always wins."

"Who are you to me?"

"I cannot tell you that, you must discover that on

your own," she says, stepping closer, so I can see we are the same height.

"Remember that when fire falls for ice, ice always wins," she states, and everything fades to black before I can ask her what that even means.

I WAKE up to the feeling of something pulling my hair. Turning my head, I see Bee sitting on my pillow, a piece of my hair in her hand, tugging on it.

"Food?" she asks, and I yawn as I reach into the cabinet above my head and grab a chocolate bar.

"Do you eat anything other than chocolate?" I ask her, and she shakes her head, pointing to the tree.

"Leaves food, chocolate food," she says.

"That's good speech," I smile at her as I open the chocolate bar and get out of bed. She flies over to her pod next to me, where I leave some pieces of chocolate for her.

"Bee, do you ever feel like everything is out of your control? Like you're playing a game, but you don't know the rules?" I ask her, resting my hand against the tree.

"No," she says, shaking her head and flying out of the pod. I hold my hand out, and she lands on it, hanging her feet over the side of my palm.

"Fate," she points at the mark on my hand as she speaks.

"What if fate is playing a dangerous game?" I ask her.

"Fate, good," she tells me, but I don't get to respond, as someone knocks on my door.

"Time to hide, Bee," I say, putting her in the pod, and she closes the door. I walk over to my door, opening it up and hiding my body behind it.

"Hey, can I come in?" Dagan asks, and I look down at my cat pajamas and back to Dagan.

"Erm, sure. I thought you would be Korbin for our run," I say, letting him in and shutting the door behind him.

"He is running a little late but will be here soon," he tells me, and then pauses looking at my pajamas.

"Cats?" he laughs.

"Don't, I couldn't find anything to wear last night when I got back," I say, and he shakes his head, reaching inside his jacket.

"I have a letter for you, kitty cat," he says.

"Don't call me that ever again," I groan, taking the yellow letter off him and going to sit on my bed. I open it up, reading a long invitation from one of the area's richest families for their daughter's mating ceremony. The estate is nearby, and prominent families always invite a royal to watch their matings. Normal dragons may mate whenever they like, but it's considered a blessing to have a royal in attendance. I can't see much danger with going, being that it's not far away.

"It's an invite to a mating ceremony, they think it's a blessing if I go, and they have my father's approval," I explain what it basically says.

"Makes sense," Dagan responds, still rolling that damn sexy lip ring between his lips.

"How does that not get removed when you shift?" I ask him, curious. I always thought about having my belly button or something pierced but I assumed dragon healing wouldn't let it stick.

"It's a long story, up to you if you really want to know," he says, leaning against the wall.

"Sure, I'm curious," I reply.

"There's a dragon that lives on Earth, who works in a tattoo parlour. He learnt how to do dragon piercings, tattoos, and all that. Anyway, we had a job to find a young, runaway dragon girl on Earth a few years back, it was one of our first assignments, actually," he chuckles as he rests against the wall and then carries on with his story.

"We tracked this girl, who was twenty, and found her with the tattoo guy, Lucak. They had fallen in love, and her parents wouldn't let them mate, so she ran away," he says.

"Did you take her back?" I ask.

"Nope, I'm not heartless. Besides, the family had told us she was in danger, which she wasn't. She was happy, and Lucak wanted to give us a gift to say thank you for keeping their location a secret. Especially considering we lost a lot of money doing so," he says.

"The lip ring?" I ask.

"Yep, he did this, and Kor's–" he goes to say and then laughs, "I likely shouldn't tell you that."

"What did he have pierced?" I ask, with a cheeky little smile.

"The night before Lucak was to do the piercing, we all had a bet, and the loser had to let us choose the piercing for him," he says.

"Korbin lost?" I fill in.

"Yep, but still not telling you what we chose," he winks at me, but I think I have a good idea what they would have chosen.

"And the tattoos? How does Lucak get them to stick to dragon skin with our healing," I ask.

"As mad as it sounds, dragonglass," he tells me.

"That's crazy and sounds painful," I say, a little shocked.

"It is, but it's not dangerous," he says.

"You have a tattoo like Korbin and Elias?" I ask and he grins, rolling the lip ring around.

"Yep, but kitty cat, I wouldn't ask to see it if I were you. That is, unless you want me to be taking a lot of clothes off," he says, making me blush.

"Anyways," I clear my throat, standing up and handing him the letter.

"It's tonight, and I'm guessing I will need all of my guards," I say as he reads the top of the letter.

"Also, we will need to leave in three hours in order to fly there and give you a few hours to get ready. So, looks like no class for you," he says.

"Some good news then," I grin.

"You and your dragon gonna be okay to fly there?" he asks, and I redirect the question to my dragon.

"*As long as mine are with us,*" she says, and I shake my head.

"She's cool with it," I say, and he nods, walking out of the room.

"See you in a few hours then, I will send Kor to guard your room," he says and walks out.

TWENTY-THREE

M y dragon lands with a loud thump on the ground, shaking the trees nearby, and causing snow from the tops to fall on top of her. She shakes it off before letting me back in her mind, pulling my human body back, and opening my eyes to find myself kneeling on the ground. Dagan and Kor land next to me, shifting back quickly, and I look to the skies to see Elias's dragon flying down. Elias roars, shifting as he lands and making it look effortless. He stands up, shaking the snow off and running a hand through his hair, before pulling a cigarette out of his leather jacket.

"Isola," Thorne says from behind me, coming out of the trees. His cloak is covered in snow. He decided to fly here earlier than all of us to scout the area for any danger.

"Where is the house?" I ask, looking around at the snow-covered trees and the suns setting in the sky. The light catches the snow, making it almost look like it is glowing, and it's beautiful.

"This way, princess," Elias says, and we walk through the woods with him leading the way. I slip on a piece of ice as we round a corner, and Thorne catches me, lifting me back up and smiling.

"Careful," he whispers, and I can see Dagan staring at us both as we keep walking. Thankfully, our surroundings seem to distract him as much as it does me. The trees clear out to a massive house, with a small farm in front of it, and a large metal wall surrounding the property with a big gate. The gate is open as people walk in, their heads covered, but it's clear they are well-off from their cloaks alone. They are all bright colours, with shiny jewels stitched into the partings. The pathway up to the house is lined with pretty white lights and a few trees and plants. The front door is open when we reach it, and the man at the door bows low for me.

"We have a room made up for you, your high-ness," the man says and turns around. Dagan puts his hand on the middle of my back, steering me into the house when I don't move, still staring in awe. The inside is amazing, with stories of dragons painted across the ceilings and all up the stairs. I can't take my eyes away from the little details, the dragon wings, the villages, and even the snow-covered trees painted on the walls. It must have taken months to paint this, for every little detail. I could spend hours searching it all to see what the story tells.

"It's stunning," I say, not exactly speaking to anyone in particular, as we reach the top of the stairs which lead to a big circular space with doors everywhere.

"Much like the princess," a woman says. I look over to see an older blonde woman walk out of a room. She bows low before stepping closer to me. She has a long gold dress on, with white crystal down the sides. Her hair is up in a complicated bun with lots of plaits and a gold flower on the side.

"This is your room, and I'm here to help you get ready," she points at the door she just left.

"Thank you. Lovely to meet you, you are?" I ask, holding out my hand. She looks at it strangely before accepting my handshake as she speaks.

"My name is Catrina Lowdane. It is my daughter, Elana's, mating ceremony today," she explains to me.

"I can't wait, and congratulations. I haven't seen a

mating ceremony in years, and they are always so magical," I comment. Actually, I'm very excited to relax and see some of the magic of Dragca. Mating ceremonies are amazing, and I hate that the last one I saw was my father's and stepmother's. It wasn't a true mating, not that anyone expected it to be. They didn't love each other, and my father was still very much in love with my mother. The mating can take place whether it's true or not, but a true mating is an honour to witness.

"Very true, princess, and we are very honoured to have you here," she says.

"The honour is all mine," I say, bowing my head and looking over at Elias. He is watching me, as are the other guys, but he gives me a little smile.

"Your guards are more than welcome to wait downstairs," she comments.

"The princess must have a guard close to her at all times, I will wait outside the room," Dagan interrupts with a firm voice.

"Of course," Catrina nods and looks back at me. "This way, please, princess."

"It's Isola, if you'd like to call me that," I offer as I follow her back to the room.

"If you wish, Isola," she says, holding the door open for me, and Dagan pulls it closed behind her.

"I have a range of dresses your father sent over, and I'm very good with hair styles, if you would like me to assist," she informs me.

"My father sent dresses?" I ask in reply, wanting to see the first gift he has bought me in a long time. Catrina points to a rack of coloured dresses, most of them are a light- or dark-blue, but there is one long red one. I automatically touch the red dress, pulling it out to admire the simplicity of the dark-red, it's low-cut and has a slit up the side.

"I'm sorry, that one wasn't sent by your father. It was on the rack before I added the others," Catrina says. I hold it up against myself, looking in the mirror and catching Catrina's eyes behind me.

"Red suits you, but I doubt the king would be happy with the ice princess wearing the colour of fire," she advises.

"That's the kind of attitude that I will never adopt, we are all dragons. Fire or ice, it's all the same. I believe it's time for people to see that though I may be an ice dragon, that does not mean I am against fire," I say definitively, and she smiles at me, nodding her head.

"You will make a good queen with that attitude," she replies. I go to the small bathroom, sliding the dress on, as well as the flat shoes Catrina hands me.

She sits me down in a chair in front of a mirror as she brushes my hair, curling bits and plaiting the top half, so it almost looks like a crown.

"Thank you, it looks amazing," I say, standing up and looking at myself in the full-length mirror by the dressing table. The red dress sticks to my body, the slit shows off my leg all the way up to my thigh, and the top of the dress is tied around my neck.

"Your father sent this also," Catrina says, stepping behind me and offering me a blue wooden box. I open it up to see a small tiara inside, with three white crystals in the middle.

"Thank you," I say, placing the box on the dressing table and taking the tiara out, sliding it into my hair.

"I will meet you downstairs, your highness. I wish to check on my daughter before the mating," Catrina says.

"Of course, thank you so much for your assistance," I smile at her.

"No need to thank me," she beams and walks out of the room. Dagan steps in after her, and I turn to see him just staring at me. His lips part slightly as his eyes drop down my body slowly, before travelling all the way back up.

"Kitty cat," he breathes out the nickname slowly, making my cheeks light up.

"Dagan," I reply quietly, and he snaps out of it, looking away from me.

"We should go downstairs, the ceremony will start soon," he flips his voice from dark and husky to cold and emotionless so quickly that I end up just smiling tightly.

"Okay," I say simply, feeling almost disappointed. I move to walk past him towards the door when he grabs my arm, stopping me.

"I know I shouldn't say it, and you likely don't want to know. And, fuck . . . I don't even want to say it, but you look absolutely beautiful," he says, leaving me speechless as he opens the door and waits for me. He won't meet my eyes as he holds the door, and I don't even know what I should say to him.

"Wow," I hear Thorne say as I step out of the room and see him near the top of the stairs. He breaks away from the wall, walking over to me.

"Thanks?" I ask, not sure how exactly to reply, and he chuckles.

"Red suits you, but not exactly what I was expect-ing," he acknowledges.

"That's something you should get used to, guys, I'm not what anyone was expecting," I say with a grin at their shocked and amused faces before walking across the hallway. I head down the stairs, seeing Korbin and Elias at the bottom, talking quietly. Elias is the first one to glance up, doing a double take and muttering something quietly as Korbin looks to where he is staring. Korbin smiles slowly, taking in my dress before meeting my eyes.

"Your highness," his deep voice comments as he bows low before standing up.

"Time to see something special," I say, wanting to get in our seats for the ceremony, and I hear Elias whisper ever so quietly.

"We already have."

TWENTY-FOUR

The outdoor ceremony takes place in the shape of a hexagram, with a raised platform in the middle, and all the people are standing in each of the six points. I stand alone with my guards, in front of them as they stand sentry behind me. I see Catrina in the point next to me, with an older man and two teenage boys behind them. There are twenty or so other people here, divided among the other points, and we are mostly silent as we wait for the happy couple. The wind blows my dress and hair to the side a little, making me shiver. It's freezing, but no one is wearing cloaks. The floor is marked with white powder that is mixed into the grass to make the outline for the shape. The platform has an arch made of three points, raised to meet at the top, and they have white flowers and little white lights wrapped around the pillars. Hanging from the middle of the archway is a small white stone, a mating stone that must be present for all matings.

"I don't know much about the stone, what is its purpose?" I whisper to Korbin, who is standing closest to me. I don't even remember the name of them.

"Dragon stones are said to be found when you need them, and can be discovered anywhere. They are said to appear when a true mating is well-deserved. When love mixes with fate," he whispers quietly, "or that's what I was told." I turn to face him, seeing my own longing reflected back in his gaze. He clears his throat, stepping back a little, and I turn away. I have to stop looking at him, at all of them like this . . . like they are mine.

"They are mine," my dragon whispers adamantly.

"You can't collect them, we have discussed this," I tell her.

"We can," she insists, and I don't reply to her.

I don't have the chance to respond anyway, as three women standing inside one of the points near us begin singing the River Song. The song is deep, beautiful, and full of magic in a way that makes you never want to stop listening to it. I watch silently as the couple we are waiting for walks out of the trees and to the archway. The woman is beautiful, with long red hair and wearing the prettiest dress I've ever seen. It's white, with gaps on her ribs, and flows out at the bottom. There are green leaves stitched up the sides, circling around her in the design and matching the green leaves that are plaited into her long hair. The man has red hair also, a leather suit on, with a green shirt. They look amazing together, but they hardly notice us watching them. They don't take their eyes off each other as they walk up to the platform. They stand in the middle, both of them staring at each other like they are seeing their whole world. It scares me that this could have been Jace and me, doing something I never really wanted. They say mating links your blood to theirs, creating a bond so deep that you never want to be away from the other person. And linking my blood with anyone, scares me. It's not only the bond that is forged in front of us and the exchange of blood, but sex is also a requirement to mating. Thank god, we are more modern now, and don't have to watch that. Jace told me of a story he read about how it was custom for royal dragons to watch the mating, the entire mating, to make sure it was valid. *So gross*. An old man steps out of one of the points, walking up the platform and stands in front of them.

"The ceremony will begin," he says once the music stops, and there's a silence that stretches.

"Please say the ancient words to each other," he says, and the woman starts off first.

"Link to the heart, link to the soul. I pledge my heart to you, for you, for all of the time I have left. My dragon is yours, my love is yours, and everything I am, belongs with you," she says, smiling when her partner leans forward and wipes a tear away from just under her eye. He repeats the same words, and then the old man pulls out a dragonglass dagger from his cloak.

"Please hold out your hands, like practiced," he says, and they both hold out their hands. The man cuts a line across the woman's palm, and then the man's before putting the dagger away.

"Light and dark, good and evil, and everything that makes us dragons, please bless this mating. We bless you," the man says.

The couple link their cut hands as we all whisper, "We bless you."

A light shines out of them, shooting up into the crystal, and it glows brightly as the couple look on in a daze. We are all silent as the light flashes once, and then bursts out in streams in every direction, leaving sparkling little light drops that fall from the sky. We all clap and cheer, and I can't help the smile that lights up my face when I see the happy couple kissing in the archway. *It was a true blessing.*

"The magic of Dragca has blessed the newly bonded. Let us dance and drink to celebrate their future happiness," the old man says, and people cheer more as I turn around to see my guards. They all are watching me, the light dropping around me must make me look strange or something, as they seem a bit dazed.

"Guys? Let's get some food? I'm starving," I say, and it snaps them out of it.

"You're always hungry, doll," Korbin is the first one to speak, and steps away from me.

"Not always, just most of the time," I shrug, walking out of the hexagon and towards the rows of food-laden tables that people are going to.

"I'm going to run a check on the left side of the party, if you can take the right?" Dagan asks Korbin, who nods, but pauses, looking between Elias and Thorne at my side.

"I will watch the princess, don't worry," Elias says, his husky tone sending shivers through me that I try to hide. *Why does his voice have to sound better than melted chocolate?*

"I'm here also," Thorne snaps.

"I can handle them both, go," I interrupt, and they all look at me with little smiles.

"I'm sure you can, doll, but give a shout if you need any help," Korbin says and walks off behind Dagan who shakes his head at him. I head for the food, filling my plate with all the amazing food they have. Thorne and Elias get their own plates, adding twice the amount of food onto theirs as I do mine. *And they say I'm always hungry?* I pick up some little white cakes with snowflakes on the top of them.

"I haven't had these since I was a child, they were my mother's favourite," I say, not really knowing if I'm talking to Thorne or Elias. It makes me almost homesick to look at the cakes. It reminds me of my mum sneaking us into the kitchen, where we would steal some of these before the cook noticed. We would run back to my room to eat them, giggling the entire time. Her laugh could light up an entire room, and then she was just gone.

"I remember these, they are called snowdrops, right?" Thorne asks me, and I nod, sliding one onto his plate.

"You should try one, they are so sweet," I say and

G. BAILEY

look away before he can reply to me. I hurriedly try to swallow the emotions that attempt to crawl up my throat. I grab an orange-looking drink off the side at the end of the buffet, and look around at the seven or so tables surrounding the little dance floor in the middle. The three singers are performing a song I don't recognise, but it's amazing mixed with the sound of the piano that one of the girls is playing perfectly.

"There," Elias nods his head at an empty table in the middle. I follow him over, taking a seat next to him, and Thorne sits on my other side.

"I forgot how amazing the home-cooked food is here," I comment, used to the snacks from the castle. Even though Jules used to cook me amazing food, it was never like this. I bite down on the quiche, and then eat some of the purple fruit pastries as I watch the people dance.

"Do you want to dance?" Thorne asks me, and Elias growls.

"We are paid to watch her, not dance and flirt with her," he snaps, and I turn to glare at him, pushing my chair out and standing up.

"I'd love to, Thorne," I say, walking away from the table and hearing Elias grumbling behind me as Thorne catches up with me. We walk into the throng

206

of dancers, and Thorne stops, looking awkward for a moment. Finally, I wrap my arms around his neck, and he slides his hands on my hips.

"You look nervous," I comment, looking up at him as we sway to the music.

"Not nervous, it's just maybe Elias is right," he states slowly. I feel him lean forward, pressing his lips ever so gently on my forehead. I don't know if they even touched me because they are gone so fast.

"That you're not paid to dance with me? Is everything you do around me because you get paid?" I demand, stopping the dance, and moving to walk away when Thorne pulls me against his body, holding me tightly to him.

"Look at me," he demands as I just let him move my body to the music. When I won't comply, his hand slides under my chin, forcing me to look into his hazel eyes.

"I'm not here because I'm paid. I'm not dancing with you because of money. I don't even know why I'm dancing with you, and that makes me nervous," he admits, his thumb slowly tracing circles across my cheek.

"I make you nervous?" I say breathlessly. *What is it about him that makes me like this?*

"You make me forget why I'm here, forget everything, and I fucking hate it as much as I like it," he says, moving his head closer to mine as I'm left feeling like all the air has left my body.

"I don't know what to say to you, Thorne," I admit.

"Nothing, I can't hear you say anything because this–" he begins to say when he is shoved out of my arms, and I fall backwards. I lift myself up to see Elias on top of Thorne, lifting his hand, and he punches Thorne straight in the face. The music dies off, the girls stop singing, and everyone gets quiet as we watch them fight.

"That was too fucking close to her," I hear Elias say.

"Jealous?" Thorne replies, his tone mocking, and nothing like I expected to hear from him. He punches Elias and jumps up. Thorne charges into Elias, and both of them smack into the stage, where the girls scream, scrambling to get out of the way.

"Stop!" I shout, running towards them as they punch each other, rolling across the stage. When I see Elias getting his daggers out of his jacket, I know this has gone too far. I hold my hands up, calling my dragon ice and shooting it at them, wrapping it around the bottom half of their bodies as they try to charge at each other. They both look in complete shock when they follow the ice covering their legs all the way back to me, and I lower my hands.

"Enough," I say, and they both growl. Elias' hands light up with fire just as Dagan gets to the stage. He jumps up on it and grabs Elias by his jacket. Elias and Thorne quickly burn their way out of their ice holds, both of them looking moments away from attempting to kill each other again.

"Take her back to the castle, Kor, I will deal with them," Dagan demands as Korbin puts an arm around my shoulders and turns me away from the guys.

"What happened?" Korbin asks as we walk towards the house. I don't have an answer for him, so I don't say anything as Catrina runs to catch up with us.

"Thank you for coming, and we won't speak of what happened. May I have a word alone with you before you leave?" she asks after bowing low, her eyes drifting to Korbin who pulls me closer to his side.

"I trust Korbin, whatever you want to speak to me about, can be spoken in front of him," I tell her gently, and she gives him a nervous look before speaking.

"The seers speak of the curses falling, and here you are, so close to your dragon guard. I will make sure no one speaks of the clear signs of how close you are to them, but I do want to warn you, princess," she says, and Korbin stands straighter, almost growling. I doubt that helps to sway her opinion of how close we all are. We are friends, I think anyway, and we certainly aren't anything more. But then I think of how Thorne looked at me as we danced, how difficult it is to take my eyes off Elias, and how much Dagan annoys me in that sexy way of his. And then there is Korbin, who is confusing and yet amazing. When these guards should be nothing to me, they are becoming everything in such a short amount of time. I feel like I've known them forever, not just the one week.

"Nothing is going on–" I argue, and she shakes her head, letting my weak sentence drift off. I doubt she would believe me anyway.

"All curses will fall, and people fall with them. I don't want to see ice dragons fall with the last of the curses. Be careful," she says and then walks past me, whispering, "with both your heart and your life." And I turn to watch her walk away, wondering how right she might be.

TWENTY-FIVE

ISOLA

"**D**amn, you have gotten quick," Korbin says as we get to the end of our run. We both take a breather, drinking from our bottles of water.

"It's been a month of running, of course, I have," I say, grinning at him. He is the only one speaking to me since the wedding. Elias, Thorne, and Dagan have gone into silent protector mode or something, because they won't talk to me. I've given up trying to figure them out, and decided to focus on my classes. I know I have a new class this morning: wild animals. The teacher cancelled all the classes up till now for some unknown reason.

"Thorne is cancelling his extra training tomorrow," he tells me, and I shake my head.

G. BAILEY

"And let me guess, we are flying all day Sunday, so Dagan doesn't have to speak to or train me?" I ask, because this is how it's been for weeks.

"Nope, we are training. I've had a word with Dagan, and he isn't coming. So, it'll just be you and me," he says and nods his head at the castle. "Come on."

"Why are they avoiding me?" I finally ask him. I have wanted to ask for weeks, but I just couldn't. I think I know the answer, that whatever happened at the wedding changed things. Made the friendships we were forming so very dangerous.

"Don't you know?" he questions sadly.

"I'm not certain, but I do kinda miss the assholes," I say with a little laugh.

"They can't be your friend, they've tried and failed. It's just how it has to be now, so everyone is safe," he tells me, not meeting my eyes.

"Then we are friends? Because you don't feel that way?" I ask, and he stops walking, tensing up as he looks at me.

"Don't ask me how I feel," he warns me, and then turns around heading towards the castle as I walk silently by him.

"I won't, but that also means you don't get to ask me," I say, trailing my eyes over his tattooed chest as his vest top, sticky with sweat, clings to him. I finally look up to see him staring at me.

"You have class, Isola, and I already know," he says firmly. I snap out of it, running up the stairs, and I look down to see him rubbing his face with his hands before following me up. I get to my room, shutting the door, and looking around to find Bee on my bed, passed out with a load of chocolate wrappers around her.

"Bee?" I sigh, stepping closer and lifting her little body off the bed. She curls into my hand as I take her to her pod and slide her inside, shutting the pod door after tucking her in. In the last month, she has learnt more words and grown more active. She seems to like making a big mess of my room and creating the little handbags she seems to have a problem with collecting. I smile as I look down at the second pod hanging from the tree. It is full to the rim with little leather bags of every colour, some with glitter stuff in them and others without. I grab my leather outfit, cloak, and boots, putting them on my bed. After cleaning up the wrappers, I get into the shower. Twenty minutes later, I leave my bedroom, seeing Dagan leaning against the wall this time. He doesn't look at me as he starts walking down the corridor. I jog to catch up with him, keeping silent as I look over his face. He is still rolling that lip ring between his lips, his blue eyes highlighting his handsome face as they slide over to look at me once, before looking away.

"Here is your class, princess," Dagan says, pointing at the door.

"When is this silent treatment going to end?" I ask, but he doesn't even look at me as he leans against the wall and stares at the floor. I shake my head, turning to go inside the classroom and shutting the door behind me. On each small round table is a little purple egg, and every table is filled except for one near the front. I take the seat, ignoring the stares of everyone else as we wait for the teacher to come. After a month of being ignored, being stared at like you have a dick drawn on your forehead becomes easy to ignore.

"Welcome, class," the old man from plant class says as he hobbles into the room, sitting down on the chair behind the desk.

"I'm sorry this class has been cancelled, but the eggs were not ready until now," he explains to us. I thought he was just ill or something. He hasn't been in plant class either, we were just told to study our plants in our room for the entire lesson each week.

"What are the eggs, sir?" a guy with black hair asks.

"Snakes, jewel snakes to be specific," he says, and several of the girls on other tables move their hands away from their eggs, looking scared. I have no idea what a jewel snake is, but normal snakes aren't that bad. I don't get why people are so scared of them. It's pointless to be scared of something that is likely more scared of you.

"They will hatch any moment, and it's your job to make them like you enough not to bite you, and then let them free in the woods. If you are bitten, you have fifteen minutes to get to the infirmary before you will pass out," he says, yawning as the sound of eggs cracking fills the room.

"If you want to fail the entire year, please run out of the room now," he says, and to my surprise, three people get up and run out, leaving about ten of us in here. I take a deep breath in the near-silent room as I stare at my egg, watching it wiggle a little before a deep crack appears near the top. The egg breaks open slowly as I observe, and then a tiny, green snake with spikes all down its back slithers out of the broken egg. I hold my hand flat on the desk as I hear some students swearing, and others speaking softly to their snakes, but I try not to look away from its tiny little eyes that watch me.

"Hello, little snake, I'm Isola, and erm . . . we

need to go outside without you biting me," I say, and the snake hisses at me, sliding across the table. I see a student get bitten by their snake out of the corner of my eye. A quick glance at the teacher tells me he is nearly asleep and not paying attention.

"Great," I mutter, looking back at my snake as someone else screams in the room. The snake gets to my hand, lifting its head as it opens its mouth. Doing the only thing I can think of, I turn my hand around and call my dragon, freezing the snake up to its neck, and it falls on its side. I pick up the frozen snake, keeping well away from the sharp hissing mouth. I stand up and see most of the students holding books out to keep their snakes away from them. I hold out my hand, freezing all the snakes' bodies, and the students slowly drop their books.

"Get them outside, and I will unfreeze them," I say, not waiting for a response from their shocked faces. I walk out of the room, seeing Dagan waiting for me. He just raises an eyebrow at the frozen snake in my hand but doesn't say anything. I walk past him, straight down the stairs to the front door, opening it up and walking outside. I walk to the trees, placing my snake down and slowly unfreeze the ice. It hisses at me before slinking away into the woods.

"Will you do mine, princess?" a guy asks

nervously, moving next to me and putting his snake on the ground as several more students wait behind me.

"It's Isola and sure," I say, unfreezing his snake and waiting for the next student to bring theirs. Everyone's small smile at me makes me think I may have a few less enemies after today.

TWENTY-SIX

"What is your plan for the rest of the day, princess?" Dagan asks me after I spent the rest of my lesson unfreezing the snakes, and then explaining what I did to the teacher. He was really impressed with my idea and said everyone has passed for team work.

"Going to the library to read," I say, and he nods.

"I will wait outside then," he says just as cold and impersonal as his very first sentence to me.

"Okay, then," I say, hating how awkward our conversations have become. We walk in silence until we get to the library, and he smiles at me.

"I wish things were different, kitty cat," he whispers.

"So, do I," I say, knowing if he wasn't a dragon guard and I wasn't a princess, this isn't how we would be. I look at him once more, meeting his blue eyes as they drag slowly over to mine. It takes a lot for me to pull away, to force myself to remember who he is, and that he is doing this for the right reasons. Dragon guards and ice dragons can never care for each other, or be anything more than people who know each other. Emotions and curses don't mix, despite how much it hurts to avoid them. I shake my head, knowing I need a good book to dive into and forget the real world for a while. Good books can shake your world, make you forget reality. That's what I need right now.

"Can I help you look for anything, child?" the older librarian asks me as I walk past her, and I pause, turning to look at her.

"Nope, I'm good, thank you," I say.

"Do you know how you can cast a curse? I was just reading a book on them," she explains her random statement, her eyes drifting to the door of the library, and I shake my head.

"Any dragon can call a curse at any time, but you must be desperate, dying, or so close to being destroyed that the curse is all you have left," she tells me.

"That's how Icahn's wife cast the dragon guard curse?"

"Yes, and all curses can be broken, they are made to be," she says, looking at the library door once more.

"Not without a heavy price," I say quietly.

"The heavy price makes it all worth it. You would never risk anything for something cheap and worthless, child," she chuckles, and then coughs a little, smoke coming out of her mouth. She must be really old, as dragons and dragon guards age differently than humans. For us, a hundred years is the same as ten years for humans after we turn twenty-one.

"Can I read this book on curses?"

"Come to me in an hour at the desk, and I will get it for you."

"Thank you, I never got your name?" I ask.

"Windlow Pakdragca, your highness," she bows slightly and walks away. I shake my head at the strange old lady. I know that the information on curses could be useful, but I really don't want to think about curses at the moment. I need to find a good book to get lost in, not a history lesson. I go straight past the romance aisle to the fantasy section, finding a book written about a world full of aliens and then looking for an empty sofa down the aisles. I walk down the middle aisle, stopping when I hear a feminine laugh.

"Elias, come on . . . you remember that night? It was so good, and you're single now. I don't see a reason not to," I hear. Stepping forward, I look down the aisle to see Elias leaning against a wall, and Lisa sliding her hands up his chest. He doesn't move, staring down at her as she kisses her way up his neck to his jaw.

"I can do that thing you like–" I hear her say, and I drop my book, the sentence reminding me of what Jace said to me that morning before he died. Elias and Lisa stop, turning to look at me, and I quickly pick up my book.

"Sorry to interrupt," I say, turning away and walking fast out of the library and towards a confused Dagan. I storm past him, hating how I feel like everything is crushing me, and I start to run towards my room.

"Isola!" Dagan shouts, but I ignore him as I keep running, and then I smack into the chest of someone. I look up, seeing only dark eyes under a cloak as a pain shooting through my stomach has me screaming. I look down, seeing the dagger on fire that he has slammed into my hip, and I gasp, falling to the floor as someone jumps over me. I roll over on my side, seeing Dagan and Elias fighting the guy. Elias grabs the guy's neck, snapping it as Dagan runs over to me.

"Hold on, kitty cat, shit, hold on," he desperately begs me, but darkness prevents me from doing anything other than closing my eyes.

CHAPTER
TWENTY-SEVEN
ISOLA

"*We will meet soon, and this will change everything. Just remember, I will make you remember,*" the girl's voice whispers to me, but everything feels icy cold, and I can't open my eyes. I don't want to move, I don't want to speak, but I manage one word.

"*Remember?*" I whisper.

"*So you can save us all, Isola. Now rest,*" she whispers back, and everything slowly fades away into darkness once more.

"Should we tell her what we did?" I hear Dagan question angrily, and a hand tightens around mine. I can't move or open my eyes, as I feel exhausted. Even though I can hear them, everything sounds as if it is getting further away.

"No, she can never know. No one can. This is a secret between us five now, no one will ever know," my uncle commands.

"It's not fair not to tell her," Elias demands, his voice terrifying.

"The world isn't fair, and if she knew what happened, you all know the price she would pay. You saved her life, just deal with it and move on," my uncle says, his voice leaving no room for argument.

"He is right, no one can know," Thorne's voice says, and then everything goes hazy again.

"NAUGHTY PRINCESS, I could do with seeing those crystal-blue eyes of yours pop open and stare at me in that sexy way of yours right about now," the deep husky voice of Elias fills my ears, and I blink my eyes open to see him sitting on a chair next to me. His blue eyes lock with mine, both of us silent as we stare at each other for a long time.

"Eli," I whisper, my voice crackling slightly with hurt as I remember Lisa all over him and then the dagger. I try to roll away, so he doesn't see me cry, and I howl out in pain from my stomach.

"Hey, doll, take it easy. No moving for a little bit

while your dragon healing does its job," Korbin says, and I turn to see him smiling at me from his seat on my other side. I take a deep breath, calming myself down a little.

"Who was the man that did this?" I ask, my voice breaking as I rub my tongue over my dry lips.

"Kitty cat, have some water, and let us sit you up a little," Dagan says from near the end of the bed. Korbin gets up, picking a pillow up from the floor and helping me sit forward. He slides it behind me, every movement sending sharp pains through my stomach. I look down at my vest top, lifting it to see the bandaged cut on my stomach. I pull it back down again as Dagan offers me a bottle of water with a straw in it. I take it off him with a small smile, drinking it as he sits on the end of the bed.

"We don't know who he was, but he had a badge with the fire rebellion symbol on his cloak," Dagan explains, and for the first time in a while, I feel frightened. They are everywhere, always out to get me. *How can I ever be safe?*

"He is dead now, you don't have to be frightened," Elias says, picking up on my emotions somehow.

"I'm not frightened of that man, I remember you killing him, Elias," I say, avoiding the point that I'm more frightened of all the other members of the fire rebellion who seem like they will never stop trying to kill me, not until they succeed. I search for my dragon in my mind, feeling her pain as she purrs against me, not strong enough yet to make that connection with me.

"You're awake?" Thorne asks as he walks into the small infirmary room and shuts the open door behind him. Thorne looks as tired as the rest of them do. They all look like they need a long sleep and a shower. I kind of hate that despite the fact it's clear they haven't slept or showered in ages, they still look hot. I bet I don't look hot. I bet I look more like a hot mess that smells.

"Hey," I say, and he smirks, wiping his hands over his face.

"Hey, Issy," he replies gently.

"Are you tired? Do you need anything?" Korbin asks after there's an awkward silence between us all.

"No, but how long have I been asleep? Is anyone looking after Bee?" I ask, and Korbin takes the bottle of water off me and puts in on the cabinet by the bed.

"You've been asleep three days, and no one can get into your room because Bee has put a ward up. I tried to tell her you're not well, but she glared at me like I'm an idiot or something," Dagan explains, huffing.

"There is plenty of food in there, and she knows where it is," I comment, not so worried about her now. She clearly knows how to look after herself.

"I don't think she is strong enough to heal this," Dagan comments, and then explains himself as we all stare. "She struggled to heal your arm, and you passed out from that. I think she needs to be older to wield enough magic to heal something like this."

"Makes sense," I say, yawning.

"I came in for a reason. There was an attack on the left side of the forest. We should check it out with the other guards," Thorne says.

"I will stay with Isola, we need to talk," Elias quickly says.

"No, we don't. You can go," I bite out.

"We do, because assuming things and ignoring others clearly isn't working out well for us," he says, and I just stare at him as I hear the other guys walk out of the room. When the door shuts, Elias moves closer, scooting to sit on the bed next to me. He places his hands on either side of my head.

"What you saw with me and Lisa–" he starts off.

"I don't want to know," I interrupt him, and he chuckles humourlessly.

"You do, don't lie to me. You know I don't like it when you lie to me."

"Eli, I can't want to know. I can't do any of this. I can't because it's impossible for us," I whisper, and he shakes his head.

"Nothing is impossible," he tells me, and I hold my breath as he starts to lean forward. Gently brushing his lips against mine at the start, Elias suddenly deepens the kiss as I let him take control. He slides his hand into my hair as pleasure shoots through me with every brush of his lips against mine until I can't think of anything other than Eli. Eli kisses me like he demands every part of my soul, and won't stop until it is his, and I don't want to fight him. I moan a little when he pulls back, getting off the bed and sitting back in his chair.

"Eli," I whisper.

"You need to rest, but that was real. That is what is between us: chemistry, magic, and fuck knows what else, but I want to find out. What Lisa was trying to do wasn't real, and I wouldn't have let it go further. I'm done letting rules fuck with my mind when it comes to you, the rules of this damn curse."

"You can't, we can't," I say, thinking of the curse. I couldn't let him lose his dragon over me. That would destroy everything between us, it would destroy him.

"Things have changed, and I will explain them one day, naughty princess," he smirks, while I'm just confused.

"What changed?" I ask, trying not to yawn, and he looks up.

"Everything," he says, and I close my eyes, drifting off to sleep with the taste of Eli's lips on mine and his smoky scent filling my senses.

CHAPTER

TWENTY-EIGHT

ISOLA

"**I**'m really okay, I can go back to my room now," I tell my uncle, who shakes his head as I lean down and pick up my coat that fell on the floor. I'm still a little weak, and my stomach still hurts, but it has healed over and is not bleeding anymore.

"Fine, stubborn child," he says, but there is a little bit of a smile as he turns to Dagan and Korbin.

"Take her to her room and keep guard. More dragon guards are being sent here by her father tomorrow for increased security. If another attack happens, I'm afraid she will have to be kept under twenty-four-hour watch at the castle," he explains, and they both nod.

"Isola, you must be more careful from now on.

230

The war is coming to a close. I have heard news that your father may have found the rebellion," he says. I'm not sure if that is a good thing, because it would mean a massive fight and fewer guards around both the castle and here.

"That's good, right?" I ask.

"Very good," he says.

"We need you on the throne, and not dead. So, stay close to your dragon guard, agreed?" he asks me.

"Alright," I say, not wanting that, but I get that my life means more than my freedom at the moment. I don't know how I would explain Bee if we had to move rooms. Everyone would find out about her then.

"It's good to see you alive, Isola," my uncle says, placing his hand on my shoulder and squeezing gently before walking out of the room.

"He is an emotional guy, that one," Korbin teases, and I shrug.

"He's lost a lot, I get it," I comment.

"Have you seen Thorne or Elias this morning?" I ask Korbin as he carries my bag of clothes out of the room, Dagan following us out.

"No, I haven't, but they will turn up," he shrugs my worries off, and I'm sure he is right.

"Why don't I go and get you some of your

favourite foods?" Dagan asks as we walk past the cafeteria.

"I'd like that," I smile, wondering what the hell changed between us all. They aren't ignoring me anymore; if anything they are always asking me how I am and wanting to do things for me. I don't really know what it is, but they feel like my friends again. I haven't spoken to Elias about the kiss yet, and I'm not sure how to bring it up with him. Or what he said has changed. I look down at my ring, turning it around on my finger and wishing I could talk to Thorne. We haven't had a moment alone, one of the others is always here. I have the feeling he wants to talk to me, I just don't know what it is about.

"So, doll, happy to get back to your classes?" Korbin asks me.

"Kinda, being sick is slightly boring, but I did get plenty of time to read," I say, proud of the five books I've read over the past week. Not so proud of the crazy amount of junk food I ate while reading, but oh well.

"I guess that's–" Korbin starts to say, before he suddenly falls to the floor, dropping my bag and holding his hands to his head. He looks up at me, his eyes burning black and fire spreading across them, as his face is contorted in pain. "Run from me," he spits out, and I shake my head.

"What is going on?" I ask, moving a step back when his hand goes to his sword.

"Isola, run and go to your father. Something is wrong, and I am being ordered to hurt you. I will follow you when I can get back in control," he says and then screams, falling on his side. I do what he says, fear filling me as I turn and run. I head down the stairs of the academy and out the doors, not seeing anyone on the way. I hold my stomach from the pain as I run down the steps and stop.

"We need to go to the castle, so I need you to take over," I whisper to her, and she roars, white mist appearing in front of me as we shift and fly straight into the sky.

"Danger," she warns me, flying faster than she usually does.

"I know, but he is our father," I tell her. She whines, but doesn't stop flying. My fear for my father and my guard mixes with her own fear as she flies through the mountains. The castle slowly comes into sight, and my dragon shoots towards it. The castle is as massive as I remember it being, with five diamond-topped towers, and the main part of the castle in the centre. There are bodies of guards on the floor, their

mouths parted in shock as their blood pools from their bodies on the stone. *What has happened here?* I grow more concerned when I don't see any dragons flying around, and when no one stops me as I land right outside the castle. I ask my dragon to let me back in control, despite her apprehension. I hold my side when I stand up in my human form, looking down to see it bleeding a little.

Everything inside me screams as I run through the doors of the castle, seeing the dead dragons lining the floors, and the sight makes me sick to my stomach. I try not to look at the spears in their stomachs, the dragonglass that is rare in this world. *Where did they get this much of it?* The more and more bodies I pass, both dragon and guards, the less hope I have that my father is okay. *No, I can't be too late, I can't lose him, too.* The once grand doors to the throne room are smashed into pieces of stone, in a pile on the floor, and only the hinges to the door hang off the walls. I run straight over, climbing over the rocks and broken stone. The sight in front of me makes me stop, not believing what I'm seeing, but I know it's true.

"Father . . .?" I ask quietly, knowing he won't reply to me. My father is sitting on his throne, a sword through his stomach and an open-mouthed expression on his face. His blood drips down onto the gold floors of the throne room and snow falls from the broken ceiling above onto his face. There's no ice in here, no sign he even tried to fight before he was killed. He must have never seen this coming because he trusted whoever killed him.

"No," is all I can think to say as I fall to my knees, bending my head and looking down at the ground instead of at the body of my father. I couldn't stop this, even when they warned me and risked every-thing. I hear footsteps in front of me as I watch my tears drip onto the ground, but I don't look up as I know who it is. I know from the way they smell; my dragon whispers their name to me, but I can't even think it.

"Why?" I ask as everything clicks into place. I should have known, I should have never trusted him.

"Because the curse has to end. Because he was no good for Dragca. Our city needs a true heir, me. I'm the heir of fire and ice, the one the prophecy speaks of, and it's finally time I took what is mine," he says, and every word seems to cut straight through my heart. I trusted him.

"The curse hasn't ended, I'm still here," I whisper to the dragon in front of me, but I know he could hear my words as if I'd just spoken them into his ear.

"Not for long, not even for a moment longer, actually. Your dragon guard will only thank me when you are gone. I didn't want to do this to you, not in the end, but you are just too powerful. You are of no use to me anymore, not unless you're gone," he says. I look down at the ground as his words run around my head, and I don't know what to do. I feel lost, powerless, and broken in every way possible. There's a part of the door in front of me that catches my attention, a part with the royal crest. The dragon in a circle, a proud, strong dragon. My father's words come back to me, and I know they are all I need to say.

"There's a reason ice dragons hold the throne and have done so for centuries. There's a reason the royal name of Dragice is feared." I say and stand up slowly, wiping my tears away.

"We don't give up, and we bow to no one. I'm Isola Dragice, and you will pay for what you have done," I tell him as I finally meet his now cruel eyes, before calling my dragon and feeling her take over.

"I wouldn't do that if I were you, princess," a cold female voice says, as a dagger is pressed against my neck from behind, and I stop the shift, knowing I would be dead before I could even get my dragon out.

. . .

"THORNE, why don't you get your crown, and then we can deal with the princess," the woman behind me demands in an overly sweet tone. Thorne smirks at me before walking over to my father, and lifting the crown off of his head.

"**W**hy?" I ask Thorne, who stands watching me as one of my father's guards handcuffs my arms behind me. The woman with the dagger moves it away from my neck, walking around me to stand next to Thorne. I didn't think I could be more shocked, but I am at seeing my stepmother's self-satisfied smile. Her long white hair is down, and she has a white leather outfit on with a white cloak. Her crown sparkles on her head in the light, very much like Thorne's does. Thorne must have dyed his hair and worn contacts; his once brown hair is now an almost white-blonde colour, and his eyes are no longer hazel, they are blue. A pale-blue like mine. He looks like an ice dragon, he might even be one. He did say he was the fire and ice heir. He doesn't speak a word, only staring at me and not moving. He's like an ice sculpture, but one I want to smash into a million pieces for betraying me. I thought he was my friend, and I trusted him. Hell, I even liked him. My dragon growls low in my mind, her anger towards him is even scarier than mine. Heartbreak and betrayal swim through my mind as I look around Thorne, seeing my father's body once more. *I've lost everything, everyone is gone.*

"I will answer that," my stepmother says, the happiness in her voice is hard to miss.

"I don't even remember your name. You're just the bitch that married my father and clearly betrayed him," I sneer, laughing at her as her eyes narrow. She walks over, slapping me hard across the face, and I fall to the floor.

"Careful now, and it's Tatarina," she says as I look up at her. The door to the left of the throne room opens, and Esmeralda walks in, her red heels clicking on the floor. Her cloak is gone, replaced with a red leather outfit much like her sister's, though hers is dripping with blood. There's blood in her red hair and splattered across her face as she smiles at me. It's a sinister smile, and when she gets close enough, her scent hits me. I didn't smell it before, she must have

239

hidden it, but I know straight away where I recognise it from.

"You bitch, you killed Jace!" I scream at her, trying to get up, but a sword pokes into my back. I turn around to see a dragon guard watching me, his sword placed on my back and threatening to pierce all the way through me. The dragon guard will protect the new royal family, and that's not me anymore. They protect the queen, my stepmother, as she holds the throne. It was never given to me, neither was the curse that comes with the crown. I imagine she plans to give it to Thorne.

"Yes, I remember well. He was not a fighter that one," she laughs, and I growl low.

"I will complete my vow, you evil bitch!" I scream. She just laughs as she walks over to Thorne and my stepmother.

"Everything is done. I will return to the academy to finish the other issues, sister," she says and then bows to Thorne.

"My king, how the crown suits you," she practically purrs.

"You are no king, just an idiot wearing a crown that isn't his," I spit out, and he narrows his eyes on me, still silent like a ghost.

"Let me tell you a story, one that will explain all

of this, and then perhaps you will watch your tongue," Tatarina says, walking closer to Thorne and resting her hand on his arm in a loving way as she stares at him.

"This is my son, a son I had with a fire dragon before I was dragged from my home to marry a king I had never even met. My son was hidden with an adoptive family I found, kept safe as I built the fire rebellion up and made the true heir an army," she says, clearly proud, and yet, I can't believe her.

"An ice dragon and fire dragon can't have a child," I say in disbelief.

"Yes, they can," Thorne finally speaks, holding out both his hands. In one hand a ball of flame appears, and in the other a sphere of ice. He smashes them together and grins at me.

"You apparently shouldn't believe everything you hear, princess," he says coldly.

"I would have given you the throne, I never wanted it! You didn't have to kill my father for it!" I shout at them both, and Tatarina laughs, looking behind me. I turn, looking to see Dagan, Elias, and Korbin being dragged into the room. They all look like they put up a hell of a fight, none of them are conscious as they are thrown onto the ground near me.

"Get the seer," Tatarina says, walking over to the guys and stopping near Elias. She moves to touch him, and I roar so loudly it shakes the ground around us, and ice spreads across the floor without me even realising I was doing it.

"You were right, it seems," Tatarina says, moving her hand away and smiling like she just won something.

"We should kill her and them, despite the price," Tatarina continues, flipping a dagger around in her hand as she walks back to Thorne.

"We cannot, not with the tree spirit blessing. I have explained this to you, mother," Thorne replies, clearly frustrated.

"Fine, we will play by the rules and stick to our plan, for now. She won't be a threat, none of them will be soon," she says. No one says a word for a long time, as I stare at my dragon guard with tears running down my face. If they die because of me, I won't be able to forgive myself. Everyone dies because of me, it never seems to stop.

"Was any of it real?" I ask Thorne, wanting to hear him admit it was fake from the start, as I look up at him.

"None of it," he says, his words cold as ice.

"I will kill you, and I promise that will be real," I threaten, and he smiles.

"I look forward to the day you try, and I get a reason to kill you," he replies, looking away as the door to my right opens. A girl, with her face hidden under a cloak walks in, her red dress moving around her as she moves towards Thorne.

"I was called," she says, her voice strangely familiar to me.

"Wipe her memory, and lock their dragons away. We will make her human, with no memory of who she is, and leave her on Earth. As for the guards, I will deal with them," Tatarina says, and I nearly choke on my fear. *Can she erase my memory of everything? Make me human?*

"NO!" I scream. Standing up, I knock the guard out of the way and try to run away when ice freezes my boots to the floor and spreads up my legs, stopping at my knees. Tears fall down my face as the woman in the cloak bows and walks over to me. I keep my eyes locked with Thorne's as the seer puts her hands on either side of my head, and whispers inside my mind.

"Forget everything."

EPILOGUE
ISOLA

"Time for school. Hurry up, you're going to be late, Isola," Jules says, and I chuckle, putting my Kindle down and standing up off the kitchen stool.

"Okay, okay. I'm going," I say and walk past her, patting her arm before running to the door. I grab my bag and slide my boots on, before leaving the house and walking to the bus stop. I stand there waiting, like I do every day, and it starts to snow, not that we weren't expecting snow at some point. The bus pulls up and I get on, walking down the aisle and stopping as I look at the three guys in the back row. One has black hair, tattoos, and is smoking; another has black hair too, and a lip ring that I watch him twist and play with between his lips. The last guy has a serious look, with dark-brown hair and a big, muscular build just like his friends. The three of them all stare at me as I slide into a seat. I don't look back at the new students, despite the fact they look familiar, which is impossible. I've lived in Barkwood, in Wales, my whole life. It's the smallest town ever. Anyone new or as good-looking as these guys are, I would definitely remember.

"Issy, have you seen the new hotties?" Melody asks as she scoots into the seat next to me. Melody and I have been friends since we were kids. With her black hair and blue eyes, she is a stunner, and a pretty good friend, too.

"Yeah, they are something," I say, and she laughs. We chat about pointless things until the bus stops outside the school, and we all get off the bus. I stop to put my phone in my bag when someone slams into my shoulder.

"Watch where you're going, princess," the guy with the tattoos says and storms past me with his friends into the school.

"Come with me, I want to ask you something," Melody says suddenly and grabs my hand, dragging me through the school. She drags me into the girl's bathroom, checking all the stalls and locking the door.

"This is going to sound weird, and trust me, it is.

But it's time you remember. They are here now, and I can't keep pretending to be a student," she says, looking around her and then staring into my eyes again.

"What the hell are you going on about?" I ask her as she walks over to me and places her hands on my head.

"I'm not Melody. I'm a seer, and I took your memory. Not by choice, but it's time you had your memories back and remember who you are. Promise me something?" she says, and I have no idea what has gotten into her crazy ass this morning. Maybe seeing those hot guys have sent her insane or something.

"You're acting crazy," I say, trying to move away, but she tightens her grip.

"Promise me you will bust my ass out of that castle, and get me away from your psycho stepbrother?" she asks. I start to get scared, and I grab at her arms to try and pull her off me.

"Let go!"

"No. Now, remember," she demands, and a white light blasts into my mind.

The End

__Wings of Fire link to Amazon...__

ABOUT G. BAILEY

G. Bailey is a USA Today and international
bestselling author of books that are filled with
everything from dragons to pirates. Plus, fantasy
worlds and breath-taking adventures.
G. Bailey is from the very rainy U.K. where she lives
with her husband, two children, three cheeky dogs
and one cat who rules them all.

(You can find exclusive teasers, random giveaways
and sneak peeks of new books on the way in Bailey's
Pack on Facebook or on TIKTOK— gbaileybooks)
FIND MORE BOOKS BY G. BAILEY ON AMAZON…
LINK HERE.

PART ONE
BONUS READ OF
THE MISSING WOLF

I'm Anastasia Noble, and shortly after moving to college, my life changed forever.

I became a familiar, bonded to a wolf for life and arrested simply for existing.

I woke up in the famous Familiar Empire community where I have to learn to bond with my wolf, or I can never leave.

Never again see those whom I love.

Bonding is my only option, if you could even call it an option, but add in familiars going missing every week, plus being stuck in a cabin with three mysterious, attractive, male familiars and their maddening animals...*this is not going to be easy.*

17+ RH

THE MISSING WOLF

LEAVING THE PAST BEHIND.

ANASTASIA

I stand still on the side of the train tracks, letting the cold wind blow my blonde and purple dip-dyed hair across my face. I squeeze the handle of my suitcase tighter, hoping that the train will come soon. *It's freezing today, and my coat is packed away in the suitcase, dammit.* I feel like I've waited for this day for years, the day I get to leave my foster home and join my sister at college. I look behind me into the parking lot, seeing my younger sister stood watching me go, my foster grandmother holding her hand.

Phoebe is only eleven years old, but she is acting strong today, no matter how much she wants me to stay. I smile at her, trying to ignore how difficult it feels to leave her here, but I know she couldn't be in a better home. I can get through college with our older sister and then get a job in the city, while living all together. *That's the plan anyway.*

We lost our mum and dad in a car accident ten years ago, and we were more than lucky to find a foster parent that would take all three of us in. Grandma Pops is a special kind of lady. She is kind and loves to cook, and the money she gets from fostering pays for her house. She lost her two children in a fire years ago, and she tells us regularly that we keep her happy and alive. Even if we do eat a lot for three kids. Luckily, she likes to look after us as I burn everything I attempt to cook. And I don't even want to remember the time I tried to wash my clothes, which ended in disaster.

"Train four-one-nine to Liverpool is calling at the station in one minute," the man announces over the loudspeaker, just before I hear the sound of the train coming in from a distance. I turn back to see the grey train speeding towards us, only slowing down when it gets close, but I still have to walk to get to the end carriage. I wait for the two men in front of me to get on before I step onto the carriage, turning to pull my suitcase on. I search through the full seats until I find an empty one near the back, next to a window. I have to make sure it's facing the way the train is going as it freaks me out to sit the other way. I slide my suitcase under the seat before sitting down, leaving my handbag on the small table in front of me.

I wave goodbye to my sister, who waves back, her head hidden on grandma's shoulder as she cries. I can only see her waist length, wavy blonde hair before the train pulls away. I'm going to miss her. *Urgh, it's not like we don't have phones and FaceTime!* I'm being silly. I pull my phone out of my bag and quickly send a message to my older sis, letting her know I am on the train. I also send a message to Phoebe, telling her how much I love and miss her already.

"Ticket?" the train employee guy asks, making me jump out of my skin, and my phone falls on the floor.

"Sorry! I'm always dropping stuff," I say, and the man just stares at me with a serious expression, still holding his hand out. His uniform is crisply ironed, and his hair is combed to the left without a single hair out of place. I roll my eyes and pull my bag open, pulling out my ticket and handing it to him. After he checks it for about a minute, he scribbles on it before handing it back to me. I've never understood why they bother drawing on the tickets when the machines check the tickets at the other end anyway. I put my ticket back into my bag before sliding it under the seat just as the train moves, jolting me a little.

I reach for my phone, which is stuck to some paper underneath it. I've always been taught to pick up rubbish, so I grab the paper as well as my phone before slipping out from under the table and back to my seat. I put my phone back into my handbag before looking at the leaflet I've picked up. It's one of those warning leaflets about familiars and how it is illegal to hide one. The leaflet has a giant lion symbol at the top and warning signs around the edges. It explains that you have to call the police and report them if you find one.

Familiars account for 0.003 percent of the human race, though many say they are nothing like humans and don't like to count them as such. Familiars randomly started appearing about fifty years ago, or at least publicly they did. A lot of people believe they just kept themselves hidden before that. The Familiar Empire was soon set up, and it is the only place safe for familiars to live in peace. They have their own laws, an alliance with humans, and their own land in Scotland, Spain and North America.

Unfortunately, anyone could suddenly become a

familiar, and you wouldn't know until one random day. It can be anything from a car crash to simply waking up that sets off the gene, but once a familiar, always a familiar. They have the mark on their hand, a glowing tattoo of whatever animal is bonded to them. The animals are the main reason familiars are so dangerous. They have a bond with one animal who would do anything for them. Even kill. And I heard once that some kid's animal was a lion as big as an elephant. But those are just the things we know publicly, who knows what is hidden behind the giant walls of the Familiar Empire?

"My uncle is one, you know?" a girl says, and I look up to see a young girl about ten years old hanging over her seat, her head tilted to the side as she stares at the leaflet in my hand. "He has a big rabbit for a familiar."

"That's awesome..." I say, smiling as I put the leaflet down. I bet picking up giant rabbit poo isn't that awesome, but I don't tell her that.

"I want to be a familiar when I grow up," she excitedly says. "They have cool powers and pets! Mum won't even let me get a dog!"

"Sit down, Clara! Stop talking to strangers!" her mum says, tugging the girl's arm, and she sits down after flashing me a cheeky grin.

I fold the leaflet and slide it into my bag before resting back in the seat, watching the city flash by from the window. I couldn't think of anything worse than being a familiar. You have to leave your family, your whole life, and live in the woods. *Being a familiar seems like nothing but a curse.*

Keep reading here…

THE MISSING WOLF

WHO WEARS A CLOAK THESE DAYS?

"Ana!!" my sister practically screeches as I step off the train, and then throws herself at me before I get a second to really look at her. Even though my sister is only a few inches taller than my five-foot-four self, she nearly knocks me over. I pull her blonde hair away from my face as it tries to suffocate me before she thankfully pulls away. I'm not a hugger, but Bethany always ignores that little fact.

"I missed you too, Bethany," I mutter, and she grins at me. Bethany was always the beautiful sister, and as we got older, she just got prettier. Seems the year at college has only added to that. Her blonde hair is almost white, falling in perfect waves down her back. Mine is the same, but I dyed the ends a deep purple. Another one of my attempts at sticking out in a crowd when I usually become invisible next to my gorgeous sister. Phoebe is the image of Bethany, and both of them look like photos of our mother. Whereas I look like my dad mostly, I still have the blonde hair. Bethany grins at me, then slowly runs her eyes over my outfit before letting out a long sigh.

"You look so pretty, sis," she says, and I roll my eyes. Bethany hates jeans and long-sleeved tops, which I happen to be wearing both. I didn't even look at what I threw on this morning. I shiver as the cold wind blows around me, reminding me that I should have gotten my coat out my suitcase on the train trip. It is autumn.

"You're such a bad liar," I reply, arching an eyebrow at her, and she laughs.

"Well, you are eighteen now, and I've never seen you in a dress. College is going to change all that." She waves a hand like she has sorted all the problems out.

"How so? I'm not wearing a dress to classes," I say, frowning at her. "Leggings are much easier to run around in, I think."

"Parties, of course," she tuts, laughing like it should be obvious. Bethany grabs hold of my suitcase before walking down the now empty sidewalk to the parking lot at the end.

"I need to study. There is no way I'm going to ace my nursing classes without a lot of studying," I tell her. Bethany took drama, and I wasn't the least bit surprised when she was offered a job at the end of her course, depending on her grades. Though she was an A-star student throughout high school, so there is no way she could fail.

"I love that you will have the same job mum did," she eventually tells me, and I glance over at her as she smiles sadly at me before focusing back on where she is walking. I remember my mum and dad, whereas Bethany is just over one year older than me and remembers a lot more. Phoebe doesn't remember them at all; she only has our photos and the things we can tell her. It was difficult for Bethany to leave us both to come to college, but grandma and I told her she had to find a future.

"I doubt I will do it as well as her...but I like to help people. I know this is the right thing for me to do," I reply, and I see her nod in the corner of my eye. I quickly walk forward and hold the metal gate to the car park open for Bethany to walk through before catching up with her as we walk past cars.

"You've always been the nice one. I remember

when you were twelve, and the boy down the road broke up with you because some other girl asked him out. The next day, that boy fell off his bike, cutting all his leg just outside our home. You helped him into the house, put plasters on his leg, and then walked his bike back to his house for him," she remarks. "Most people wouldn't have done that. I would have just laughed at him before leaving him on the sidewalk."

"I also called him a dumbass," I say, laughing at the memory of his shocked face. "So I wasn't all that nice."

"That's why you are so amazing, sis," she laughs, and I chuckle as we get to Bethany's car. It's a run down, black Ford Fiesta, but I know Bethany adores the old thing. Even if there are scratches and bumps all over the poor car from Bethany's terrible driving.

"Get in, I can put the suitcase in the boot," she says, and I pull the passenger door open before sliding inside. I do my seatbelt up before resting back, watching out of the passenger window at the train pulling out of the station. There is a man in a black cloak stood still in the middle of the path, the wind pushing his cloak around his legs, but his hood is up, covering his face. I just stare, feeling stranger and more freaked out by the second as the man lifts his head. I see a flash of yellow under his hood for a brief moment, and I sit forward, trying to see more of the strange man I can't pull my eyes from. I almost jump out of my skin when Bethany gets in the car, slamming her door shut behind her, and I look over at her.

"Are you okay? You look pale," she asks, reaching over to put her hand on my head to check my temperature before pulling it away. I look back towards the man, seeing that he and the train are gone. Everything is quiet, still and creepy. *Time to go.*

"Yeah, everything is fine. I'm just nervous about my first day," I tell her, which is sort of honest, but I'm missing the little fact about the weird hooded man. *I mean, who walks around in cloaks like friggin' Darth Vader?* She frowns at me, seeing through my lies easily, but after I don't say a word for a while, she drops it.

"It will be fine. Don't worry!" she says, reaching over to squeeze my hand before starting the car. I keep my eyes on the spot the man was in until I can't see it anymore. I close my eyes and shake my head, knowing it was just a creepy guy, and I need to forget it. This is my first day of my new life, and nothing is going to ruin that.

THE MISSING WOLF

ONE MOMENT CAN CHANGE EVERYTHING.

"Anastasia Noble?" I hear someone shout out as I wait in the middle of the crowd of new students. Bethany left me here about half an hour ago, and she is going to find me later once I have my room sorted. First, I have to get through a tour of the university, even though I had a tour here when I visited two months ago. I also spent days studying the map they gave me, so I know where I am going. Putting my hand in the air, I move through the crowd, pulling my suitcase behind me with my arm starting to ache from lugging the giant purple suitcase everywhere.

I get to the front of the crowd, where an older man waves me over. I quickly make my way to him and the three other students waiting at his side. Two of them are girls, both blonde and whispering between themselves with their pink suitcases. The other is a guy who is too interested in ogling the blondes to notice me coming over. Story of my life right there. I stop right in front of the older man who stinks of too much cologne, and I shake his slightly sweaty hand before stepping back.

"Welcome to Liverpool University. We are the smallest, but fiercest, university in northern England. Now, I am going to show you around the basic area before taking you to your rooms. You all will share a corridor and living area, so look around at your new friends and maybe say hello!" the man says, clapping his hands together before quickly turning to walk away. We all jog to catch up with him as he walks us across the grass towards one of the buildings on either side of the clearing.

There is a little river in the middle with planted flowers and trees all surrounding it. It's peaceful, exactly why my sister chose this university, I suspect. She always likes seeing the beauty in life, where I am always looking for a way to fix the world instead. I wish we had other family around that could tell us about what our parents were like, who each of us follow, or if we are just random in the family line of personalities. We don't even know if our parents had any close friends. There is nothing much in our foster pack given to grandma from social services. Bethany and I talked about going to the village we lived in to ask around, but neither of us ever found the time.

"Anastasia, right?" a guy asks, slowing down to walk at my side. He has messy brown hair, blue eyes, and a big rucksack on his back.

"Yep, who are you?" I ask.

"Don. Nice to meet you," he replies, offering me a hand to shake with a big grin. I shake his hand before looking up at the massive archway we are walking through to get inside of the building. It is two smooth pillars meeting together in the middle. There are old gargoyle statues lining the archway, their creepy eyes staring down at me. Those statues always creep me out. Bethany thinks it's funny, so last Christmas, she got me gargoyle romance books as a joke. Jokes on her though; some of those books were damn good. I quickly look away, back to where we are walking, as Don starts talking again.

"I've heard there is a party tonight to welcome freshers. Are you going?" he asks me, his arm annoyingly brushing against mine with how closely he has decided to walk. I glance up at him to see his gaze is firmly focused on my breasts rather than my face.

"No. I need to unpack," I curtly reply.

"Can't it wait one night?" he asks, and I look over at him once again. He is gorgeous, but the whiney attitude about a party is a big turn off. "I will make sure you have fun."

"No. It can't wait, and I doubt anything you could do would make the party fun for me," I say honestly, and not shockingly, he nods before catching up with the two blonde girls in the group, trying his pickup techniques on them. *Men.*

Bethany says I'm picky, but actually, it's just because the general male population at my age are idiots and act like kids most of the time too. I don't see how anyone could want to date them, though Bethany is on her twelfth boyfriend since she came to college, so I know she doesn't share my opinion. She swears she will know when the right guy comes along, and it will be the same for me. I doubt it. Anyway, finding the "right" guy is not the most important thing at the moment; passing college and getting my nursing degree is.

"This is the oldest part of the university and where most the lessons are. In the welcome packs sent to your old homes were the links to an app which is a map. It will help you find your lessons," the tour guide explains before opening a door out of the old corridor and into another one which is more modern. There are white-tiled floors, lockers lining the walls, and spotlights in the ceiling that shine so brightly everything gleams. "Every student gets a locker here, which is perfect for storing books and anything you don't need for every class. Trust me, you will get a lot of books, so the lockers are a godsend."

We walk down the corridor, listening to the guide explain the history of the university when suddenly there is a burning feeling in my hand that comes out of nowhere. I scream, dropping to my knees as I grab my hand, trying to stop the incredible pain. I rub at my pale skin as it burns hot, yet there is nothing there to see. The pain gets worse until I can't see or hear anything for a moment, and I fall back. When I blink my eyes open, I'm lying on the cold floor, hearing the chatter of students near me. No one is helping me, oddly enough, and they sound like they are far away. Every part of my body hurts, aches like I've been running a marathon.

"She's a familiar. Has anyone called the police?" one person asks as I stare up at the flickering spotlight right above me.

"We should leave; she could hurt us. Who knows where her creature is!" another man harshly whispers. I lift my hand above my face almost in slow motion.

My eyes widen in pure shock at the huge, glowing, purple wolf tattoo covering the back of my hand where it burned. It stops at my wrist, the wolf's fur extending halfway up my fingers and thumb. The eyes of the wolf tattoo glow the brightest as I realise what this means.

"I'm a familiar."

THE MISSING WOLF

TIME TO RUN BEFORE IT IS TOO LATE.

As soon as I've said it out loud, it feels like I can't breathe as I sit up and look around at the people staring at me. The group I was with are huddled by the lockers a good distance away from me now, and I turn to see more people have shown up, a few of them on their phones. All of them are scared, worried what I will do as they keep their eyes on me. They are going to call the police and have me taken away because of this. *I have to get to Bethany first.* I have to at least say goodbye to her before they come for me and take me some place where I may never see her again.

I quickly scramble to my feet and run down the

corridor, passing everyone who shouts for me to stop, until I get to the door at the end. I push it open, running through the arch and into the empty clearing. Stopping by the river, I look up and quickly try to remember how to get to the dorms. Shit, I don't even know what room she is in. I pull my handbag off my shoulder to get my phone out just as I hear a low growl from right behind me.

I slowly drop my bag onto the floor and turn around, seeing a giant wolf inches away from my face. The wolf is taller than I am; its head is leant down so I can see into its stunning blue eyes. They remind me of my own eyes, to be honest, with little swirls of black, light and dark blues, all mixed together. My body and mind seem to relax as I stare at the creature, one which I should be terrified of...but I am not. I feel myself moving my hand up, and then the wolf growls a little, shaking me out of that thought.

I step back, which only seems to piss her or him off more. Some deep part of me knows I have to touch the wolf now, or I will always regret it. I take a deep breath before stepping closer and quickly placing my hand on the middle of the wolf's fore-head. I didn't notice it was my hand with the familiar mark on it until this point, until it glows so brightly purple that I have to turn my head away. When the light dims, I look back to see the black wolf staring at me as I lower my hand.

"Your name is Shadow," I say out loud, though I don't have a clue how I know that, but I know it is true. Shadow bows his head before lying on the ground in front of me. He is my familiar. *That's how I know.* That's why I am not scared of the enormous wolf like I should be. I have a gigantic wolf for my familiar. *Holy crap.* It takes me a few seconds to pull my gaze from Shadow and remember what I was going to do. Find my sister, that's what.

"We need to find my sister…can you help me? Like smell her, maybe? She smells like me," I ask Shadow and then realise I have no clue if he can understand me. Shadow looks up, tilting his head to the side before stretching out, knocking his head into my stomach. I step back, sighing. "Never mind."

Shadow growls at me, and I give him a questioning look. What is up with the growling? I thought familiar animals were meant to be familiars' best friends or something. I really get the feeling Shadow isn't all that impressed with me. He shakes his giant head before walking around me and slowly running off in the direction of the other building.

"Wait up!" I have to run fast to catch up with him

as he gets to the front of the university, people moving fast out of his way and some even screaming. I don't even blame them. A giant black wolf running towards you is not something you see every day. I run faster, getting to Shadow's side as we round a corner, and I hear Bethany's laugh just before I see her sat on a bench with a guy. They both turn with wide, scared eyes to us, and the guy falls back off the bench before running away.

The sounds of people's screaming, shouting and general fear drift into nothing but silence as I meet my sister's eyes as she stands up. A tear streams down her cheek, saying everything neither one of us can speak. I will be made to leave her, and I have no idea when—if ever—I will get to see her again. Bethany is the first to move, running to me and wrapping her arms around my shoulders. She doesn't even look at Shadow; she doesn't fear me either, which is a huge relief. I hug her back, trying to commit every part of her to my memory as I try not to cry. *I have to be strong*. If I break down now, Bethany will never be able to cope. I pull back as I hear sirens in the background and know my time here is coming to an end.

"I will find a way back to you. I will never stop until I do. Just look after yourself and Phoebe.

Promise me?" I ask Bethany, holding my hands on her shoulders as she sobs.

"I promise. If anyone can work out a way around the rules, it's you. I love you, sis," she says, crying her eyes out between each word. I hug her once more before stepping back to Shadow's side, away from my sister and my old life. "Be safe."

"Go. Just go, I don't want you to see me arrested or how nasty the police are to familiars. The YouTube videos are enough," I say, but Bethany shakes her head, wiping her cheeks and crossing her arms. I've accidently seen enough videos online to know that the police, the government and the general population are not nice to new familiars. That's why they are taken straight away. I'm not going to fight or try to run like some familiars do. I doubt I would get far with Shadow at my side.

"I am staying until they take you. You will not be alone," she says as I hear shouting and the sounds of dozens of feet running towards us. I gasp as I feel a sharp prick in the side of my neck, and Bethany screams. Shadow growls, which turns into a howl as I try to reach for him as he falls to the ground at my side. The world turns to blackness, and the last thing I hear is Bethany's pleas for someone to leave me alone.

THE MISSING WOLF

NEW LIFE. NEW WORLD.

I cough as I wake up, my throat feeling dry and scratchy as I look up at the wood ceiling above me. The smell of fire and smoke fills my nose, making me lift my hand to rub it as I sit up. A red blanket falls to my lap as I look around the cabin I am in. Shadow is lying on the floor near a window, his eyes watching me closely, and the rest of the room is just a row of beds like the one I am in. There is a fireplace on the far wall, where the smell of burning wood is coming from. I look out the window Shadow is lying under, seeing frost covered trees. It wasn't frosty in Liverpool the last time I checked. Where have they taken me? Surely, I haven't slept the entire way to the

Familiar Empire…but the evidence is looking like that is likely.

I slip my legs out of the bed, seeing that I'm still wearing the clothes from my first day at university, but they are wrinkled now, and the jeans are dirty with mud. There is a glass of water on the bedside unit and a little note. I pick the water up and take a sip before drinking it all quickly once I realise how thirsty I am. I put the glass down and pick up the note, hastily reading it.

Welcome to your new home, the Familiar Empire.
The door by the fireplace leads to a bathroom, and a
spare outfit is in there for you from your suitcase.
Clean up and come outside. R.

I put the note back down and stare over at Shadow, remembering Bethany's pleas before the police—I presume—knocked me out. There is no going back now. I'm a familiar, and my life as I knew it is over. Grandma Pops always said you have to make the best of a bad situation because giving up is not an option. That is what I am going to do. I can fix this…*somehow.* I slide off the bed, walking past Shadow, who watches my every movement before getting to the door near the fireplace. I push it and walk inside, closing the door behind me.

The bathroom smells of bleach, but I guess that means it's clean at least. It's colder in here, and its basic design is something you would see in any hotel. There is a shower, towels on a shelf nearby, and a standard toilet and sink. I quickly use the toilet before washing my hands and looking around for the clothes. On a wooden laundry box in the corner is a pile of clothes, as the note mentioned. I pick them up, seeing ripped jeans and a blue jumper. This is one of my favourite jumpers, so I'm glad they picked that, especially considering the frost covered trees outside. I mentally catalogue all the clothes I have in my suitcase and know that not a lot of them are suitable for cold weather. I had saved up money for college, and there was little else left. Plus, Bethany assured me she had winter clothes I could borrow. *Dammit.* There is also a pink bra and matching knickers under the pile. I don't want to know who went through my suitcase and picked these; I can only hope it was a girl. By the simple fact they are a matching set, I'm willing to bet it was.

I put the clothes back and carefully pull off my dirt covered clothes. I leave them all in a pile by the sink, and as I glance up, I see my reflection in the small mirror. My hair is messy, sticking in all directions, and my skin is pale. There are big bags under my eyes, even though I've clearly slept for a long time, and my blue eyes now only remind me of Shadow and how similar they are.

I grip the sink, looking down and breathing in deep breaths. I'm a familiar. I wish I had learnt more about their kind growing up, but I never suspected I would be one of them. Only 0.003 percent of the entire human race are. *What are the chances I would be one of them?* I breathe in and shake my head once again. I know I need to shower and face the world I am now a part of. I only have to make my shaky legs move first.

It takes a few seconds before I can let go of the sink and walk the few steps to the shower. I step back as I switch it on, knowing there is a good chance cold water is going to come out first. Knowing me, I'd end up jumping back and knocking myself out somehow. I put my hand out and test the water, waiting for it to go warm before finally stepping in. Resting my head under the warm water, I let it soothe me before opening my eyes, seeing hotel-like little bottles on a shelf in front of me. I'm curious about this place, so I quickly wash my hair and myself before getting out the shower.

Lacking a hair dryer and my brush, I towel dry my hair as much as possible before running my fingers through it. It feels good to pull my clean clothes on, and I fold the towels up, not wanting to leave a mess. Going back to the mirror, I glance at myself one more time, knowing I need to walk out of here with my head lifted high. I'm Anastasia Noble, and I am familiar. The more I repeat it, the more it sinks in. This is my life now.